JACKIE
WON A PONY

Judith M. Berrisford

D1352434

Armada

First published in the U.K. in 1958 by
Brockhampton Press Ltd., Leicester. This edition
was first published in Armada in 1970 by Fontana Paperbacks,
14 St. James's Place, London SW1A 1PS.

This impression 1978.

© 1958 Judith M. Berrisford

Printed in Great Britain by Love & Malcomson Ltd.,
Brighton Road, Redhill, Surrey.

CONTENTS

CHAPTER ONE

PONY-MAD—AND PONYLESS

I'D WON a pony! I simply couldn't believe it.

Breathlessly I kept telling myself the staggering news as I hurried along the garden path, reading again the letter which the midday postman had just handed me. This time I read every word on that sheet of paper.

HORSESHOES

Underneath were small sketches of cantering riders and a border of horseshoes.

Then came the address and telephone numbers of *Horseshoes*, and the words: Britain's Premier

Weekly for Pony-Lovers, followed by the date, and—

Dear Jacqueline,

You will, I am sure, be delighted to learn that the judges of our recent competition for the best essay on IF I WON A PONY *have awarded you the first prize of a pony.*

If you would telephone me at this office— reverse the charge—I should be very happy to make arrangements for you to choose your pony prize.

Yours sincerely,

Stephen Clarke,

EDITOR

Miss Jacqueline Hope,
Cherry Trees,
Marston-near-the-Sea.

After the first wild excitement, I suddenly felt quite weak, so I sank on to the garden seat and looked again at the letter while my numbed brain struggled to take in the stupendous news.

For years I'd been pony-mad and ponyless. How I'd dreamed of owning a pony! But like lots of other girls I'd had to be content with rides on friends' ponies. Sometimes I would hire ponies from local riding stables whenever I had enough pocket money.

And to think my essay had won a pony! I

tried to remember what I'd written. Oh, yes, I'd said how much I'd longed for a pony. I'd described just how I'd look after the pony if I won. I explained about the empty paddock at Cherry Trees, with its white-painted railing, good grazing, and leafy chestnut trees where a pony might find cool shade on a sunny day.

I suppose part of the idea of the essay was to enable the judges to be sure that they were giving a pony to a girl who would be able to look after it properly, and have plenty of grazing and room for it, and whose parents would be willing for her to keep a pony. I suppose that was why, when I sent in my entry, my parents had to sign a form, stating that they were willing for me to have a pony.

Wouldn't my parents be thrilled when they heard the news? I decided to write to them straight after breakfast. Both Mummy and Daddy were in Greece, 'digging' for relics of past civilizations. Daddy, by the way, is a history lecturer at a university. He and Mummy had gone to Greece at the beginning of the long summer holidays, and I'd been sent here to the New Vicarage, Cedar Avenue, Frensham, about fifty miles from Cherry Trees, to stay with Aunt Alice and Uncle James, and my cousin, Babs, who is just six months younger than me. I'm nearly fourteen.

Suddenly I caught sight of the address on the

envelope. It had been redirected by one of the Torrence tribe from Cherry Trees. Since our house was only a couple of miles from the sea, Mummy and Daddy had no difficulty in letting it furnished for the summer months, while they were 'digging'. Some people named Torrence had answered the advertisement. So the Torrence family—including the three teenagers, June, Sally and Pete—were now in residence. I was sure that they wouldn't mind my keeping the pony in the paddock while they were Daddy's tenants. In fact they would probably love it. They were probably just as pony-mad as I was. Perhaps they would ask me to stay at Cherry Trees so that I could be near the pony.

Scamp, my golden cocker spaniel, galloped down the path towards me. He sniffed the letter, and wagged his tail, then he dabbed wet kisses on my cheek as I bent to pat him.

"Yes, Scamp," I told him. "It's good news, because you'll like the pony. It will be company for you when I'm at school. And you need never be jealous. I'll still love you just as much as ever."

"Woof!" agreed Scamp, not understanding a word, of course. But he understood what I next said: "Where's Babs?"

Scamp dashed off to lead me to my cousin. His long ears flapped as he ran down the path and round the side of the modern vicarage—oh,

I forgot to tell you that Uncle James is really the Reverend James Maitland Spencer, M.A., Vicar of All Saints, in the parish of Frensham. Babs is short for Barbara Ariadne Bettina Spencer, which is far too dignified for a girl like Babs. Anyhow she wasn't called that for long. Even in a vicarage you could never call Babs by anything but a pet name. And quite apart from *BABS* being short for Barbara, it's also what her initials spell.

Scamp tracked Babs down to the cycle shed where she was cleaning her bike.

"Look!" I said, handing her the letter with a flourish. "Read that!"

"Oh, Jackie!" she exclaimed, and I could see that she was just as happy and excited as I was. "How simply super! May I come with you to choose the pony?"

"Of course!"

CHAPTER TWO

WHICH PONY FOR ME?

PONIES, ponies everywhere and one of them would be mine.

A few days later I followed in dazed silence while Gwen, the show-jumping daughter of Mr Murrow, showed us round Green Paddocks. There were four of us looking at the ponies—Stephen Clarke, the young editor of *Horseshoes*, and his nephew, Dick Clarke, who was an up-and-coming show-jumper. Lastly there were Babs and me. We were there to choose my prize pony.

Even Babs was awed into silence by the horsey splendour around us. Green Paddocks was an elegant house with a range of stables surrounding a courtyard. A little farther away were still more stables, and then rows of loose-boxes.

In every loose-box were ponies.

Yes, ponies, ponies—and still more ponies!

We had already looked at about twenty and we were only just starting on the second stable block. There had been blacks, bays, chestnuts, greys, skewbalds, a dun and a very fine liver chestnut. I just did not know which to choose.

Gwen Murrow opened the door of the next building and, as we went slowly along the passage, pony heads turned to look at us through the loose-box bars.

"This is a promising show-jumper," Gwen announced, opening the door of one of the loose-boxes, and leading us to see the cobby bay inside. "He's named Firecracker, and he's a fine jumper."

Mr Stephen Clarke eyed me quizzically; then he glanced at the bay who was moving restlessly on the cobbles.

"Jackie might find him even more fiery than his name if that's possible." He turned to me. "What do you think, my dear? Could you manage him?"

"Jackie can manage anything on four legs!" Babs said loyally before I had the chance to reply.

"Perhaps," I said doubtfully, aware that all eyes—including the ponies'—were turned on me. "But I wouldn't want to spoil a promising show-jumper if it so happens I'm not good enough to ride him."

Mr Clarke's nephew, Dick, moved to my side.

"Very wise," he nodded, giving me a friendly smile. "I think you ought to choose a well-

13

schooled pony that's got enough *go* but not too much. Then your pony will help you to be a good rider. Choose a 'hot' pony like Fire-cracker and you might spoil him and he could ruin you as a rider.'

"There's a lot in what you say, Dick," Mr Clarke nodded, and we all moved towards the next pony.

"Meet Greensleeves." Gwen Murrow intro-duced us to a gentle-eyed mare. "She used to be a polo pony. She has a mouth like velvet, and she's willing and keen. She's also quiet in traffic and stable."

Greensleeves was a chestnut with a flaxen mane and tail. I patted her neck and she made a whickering noise as though she liked me. She had a kindly eye and she stood quietly and con-tentedly, watching us out of sight. Was she just a little sad as we moved away?

"This is Romany," Gwen told us, showing us a strawberry roan. "She's a good gymkhana pony—not 'hot' though. Just right for an inex-perienced rider. She'll carry you anywhere. She's got enough spirit to enter into the fun of things, and yet she's willing and obedient."

I looked at the keenly pricked ears, the gentle eyes and powerful hocks. Romany was a good pony, sure enough.

Then there was Damson, dappled-grey, and Tulip, velvety black and a winner in showing classes; Harmony, a sweet-faced bay with black points; and Barbecue, a lively chestnut with mischievous ways. I could have given my heart to

any of them. I looked helplessly at Babs as we came to the end of the loose-boxes.

I felt just the same as when I'd caught my first glimpse of the ponies. Ponies, ponies, everywhere—but which was the one for me?

"They're all so wonderful," I said, hoping I didn't look too bewildered and wondering how I could possibly make up my mind.

"Let's go and have tea in the town," Stephen Clarke invited understandingly. "And then you can think it over."

"Yes; decide which *three* you like best," Gwen Murrow suggested. "And then come back after tea and try them out. I'll have the schooling paddock ready."

"You lucky thing, Jackie," Babs sighed. "Everything laid on for you except the red carpet. There isn't a pony-mad girl in Britain who wouldn't envy you at this moment."

CHAPTER THREE

I FIND MISTY

AFTER tea and cream cakes at an olde-world tea-shoppe at Market Wainbury, Mr. Stephen Clarke and I were standing on the pavement, waiting for Babs. She had gone back to look for her mac-belt which she had dropped somewhere in the café. Mr Clarke's nephew, Dick, wasn't with us. He hadn't joined us for tea. He couldn't be dragged away from the ponies.

I'd decided on trying out Damson, Romany and Greensleeves, and, of course, my mind was full of ponies. That's why it didn't seem strange at first when I heard a soft whinny nearby, despite the fact that we were a mile or so away from the stables.

Then my thoughts came right back to where I was—near the Butter Cross outside the olde-worlde tea-shoppe—as I heard hooves clip-clopping round the corner towards me.

Mr Clarke and I turned our heads at the same moment, and saw a grey Welsh mare, with a

17

black mane and tail, walking forlornly towards us. She was pulling a cart loaded with firewood.

She looked straight into my eyes and came on walking until she was standing in front of me, as though inviting me to make a fuss of her.

My first sight—and stroking—of Misty! I'll never forget it. Odd how things happen. I came to choose a pony, but instead it was as though she was the one who did the choosing.

"Hello, beauty!" Mr Clarke was saying. "Playing truant? Where have you left your owner?"

"Maybe she's looking for a new owner." I'm not sure whether I said that, or just thought it. Anyway I added: "I wonder how such a lovely pony came to be pulling firewood."

Mr Clarke pointed to a scar on the pony's off-fore.

"She might have been a show pony until that healed scar spoiled her appearance," he suggested. "But that scar's really nothing. She looks absolutely sound."

Just then a dark young man, in a light brown trilby and a red scarf, came round the corner.

"Ho, so you're making friends again—begging for sugar, are you?" the young man said to the mare, and smiled at me. "Don't mind Misty. I reckon she thinks she knows you, missy. You'll be putting her in mind of the young lady she used to belong to—one of them show-riding young ladies she was." He paused. "It's quite a story in a manner of speaking."

"Go on," I said eagerly. "What happened?"

"Well, one day she took Misty out hunting, and put her at a hedge where there was barbed wire," the young man explained. "Misty got this cut—yes, where the scar is—and the young lady took a bad fall and broke her leg. She lost her nerve after that. Misty went to a dealer, and then I bought her."

"Nobody else would buy her because of that scar, I suppose," I said.

"That's about the size of it," the young man nodded. "They thought it spoilt the look of her."

"Poor Misty!" I murmured, and the pony put her velvet-soft muzzle against my cheek as though to thank me for my understanding.

"Misty Morn was her full name," the young man explained. "But it seemed a bit fancy for a pony that pulled a cart, so I just called her Misty."

Just then Babs came out of the café, triumphantly waving her mac-belt.

"If I promised to give this pony a good home," I impulsively said to the young firewood dealer, "would you sell her to me?"

"Good gracious!" exclaimed the editor of *Horseshoes*.

"Whatever are you up to, Jackie?" Babs demanded.

Meanwhile the young man thought about my offer and looked from Misty to me, and back again to Misty.

"Now that's a proper poser." He pushed back his trilby and ruffled his dark, gypsy-like curls. "I'm fond of Misty, but I wouldn't stand in her way, especially as I think she'd rather belong to a young lady. She looks proper sad sometimes pulling this cart. Folks feel sorry for her, and some even think I can't be treating her right. But I do."

"I'm sure you do," I agreed.

"I gave thirty pounds for her," he added cautiously.

"And you'd take forty for her now?" Mr Clarke suggested.

"Yes, I would," the young man agreed. "That's if you felt this lady was doing the right thing."

"Well, are you?" Mr Clarke turned to me.

"I am. I'm sure I am." I put my arms round Misty's neck. "I won a pony, and I do so want it to be this one."

As Mr. Clarke and the firewood-dealer were fixing up the details, I faced a barrage of questions from Babs.

I cut across them by saying: "I suppose you think I'm rather soppy and quite mad."

"Maybe I do!" she declared. "But I'm sure of one thing."

"What's that?"

"I'd have jolly well done the same myself!"

Then Babs was hugging Misty, and petting and stroking her to show that she had fallen in love with her just as much as I had.

CHAPTER FOUR

FULL HOUSE

AFTER that things happened fast.

"When d'you want to take Misty?" the youth had asked.

"Right away," Babs answered for me.

I nodded. Cherry Trees was only a few miles from Market Wainbury. I could ride Misty home that evening and put her in the paddock. As I've explained, the Torrences, who had rented Cherry Trees while Mummy and Daddy were away, were a friendly family, and I felt fairly sure that my idea of camping out in the orchard or even sleeping in the attic to be near my prize pony, would fit in with their plans. I arranged to collect Misty from the firewood yard at six o'clock, and, in the meantime, Mr Clark took Babs and me to choose a saddle and bridle for her. She'd go well in a snaffle, he thought, and we bought her a lovely bridle.

22

"You'd better have a show-jumping saddle," Mr Clarke advised.

Babs nodded eagerly.

"I don't suppose I'll ever be good enough to show jump," I said.

Mr Clarke laughed. "Better be prepared anyhow," he said. "First it'll be gymkhanas. Next the show ring. You'll catch the fever."

Later Mr Clarke went off to break the news about Misty to the Murrows and to collect his nephew, Dick.

Babs and I went to telephone the Torrences. We tried three times, but the number was engaged.

"Never mind," I said. "We'll arrive without warning them. Misty will be a pleasant surprise for them."

When we went to pick up Misty, Mr Clarke and Dick were waiting at the firewood yard with Gwen Murrow who had come to check that the pony was sound.

Misty was ready saddled and bridled, and she was enjoying all the fuss while Gwen inspected her from all angles.

"She's a splendid pony," Gwen declared. "I'm glad you picked her, Jackie. She deserves a good home."

I took up Misty's reins and mounted. The new saddle felt slippery, but Misty's back was comfortable.

"Good luck," said Mr. Clarke. "Let me know how you get on. *Horseshoes* expects big things of you, Jackie. I had great difficulty to get the directors to agree to our giving a pony prize, so don't let me down."

"I won't," I promised cheerfully.

I rode Misty out of the firewood yard, and pointed her head towards Cherry Trees and the Downs.

Misty stepped out proudly, playing with her bit and tossing her head. She seemed to know that her cart-pulling days were over. Her eyes were bright as we left the town behind and came on to the open country of the Downs.

Soon we were cantering easily towards the sea, and there, in a hollow, I could see the green roof tiles of Cherry Trees.

"Nearly home," I told Misty, thinking how pleased she would be when she was turned into the empty paddock to stand in the shade of the big chestnut tree and to crop the sweet turf, and eat the windfall apples where the orchard trees overhung the paddock fence.

I walked Misty for the last half-mile so that she would cool off after the ride. At last we came in sight of the paddock.

Goodness! What was happening?

I reined up and blinked in amazement. There in the paddock — *our* paddock — were four ponies: two greys, a chestnut and a bay. The

two Torrence girls, June and Sally, were un-
saddling one of the ponies while Pete Torrence
and another boy knocked in nails as they put
up a wooden jump.

"Hullo, Jackie!" June, the elder of the two
Torrence girls, smiled as I rode Misty to the
paddock gate. "It's grand to see you—and what
a lovely pony!"

"I've brought Misty to join the party," I explained.

"What do you mean?" asked Sally. "If you
want her to stay here for the Rally, it'd be grand

to have you and her, of course, but there simply isn't any room."

I explained about the pony prize and my choosing Misty.

"There's nowhere to keep her at Uncle James's where I'm staying," I told them. "It's a modern vicarage with only a small garden, and it's in a built-up area. That's why I brought Misty here. I thought she could stay in the paddock, and you could ride her."

"We'd have been glad," June said warmly. "But we've hired these ponies for the summer. As it is there just isn't enough grazing."

"Never mind. I'll probably be able to keep Misty at one of the nearby farms," I decided.

"I doubt it," said Pete, who had come to join the group. "You see, there's the Horse Club Rally—it's on all week. When we knew what good riding country this was we suggested to our local Horse Club that we should have a Rally, and so every possible inch of grazing has been spoken for. We've got three friends and their ponies coming this evening."

I felt desperate. "Well, may I put Misty in the orchard for to-night?" I asked. "Then to-morrow I could find somewhere for her to go. It's rather late to start looking for anywhere now."

"Oh, yes; that should be all right," June agreed. "Would you mind sleeping on the sofa?

I'm afraid all the beds are full. We've even got a couple of cousins in your attic. What bad luck for you, Jackie."

"I know!" Sally suddenly said. "Let's unsaddle Misty. Then you might start 'phoning round to see if you can find any grazing. Supper shouldn't be very long. Mother's just waiting for everybody to arrive before she starts dishing up."

How sweet home would have been if there'd been any room for Misty and me! Saddles and bridles were all over the hall. Betty and Linda, the Torrences' cousins, in check shirts, jeans and pony-tail hair-dos, were setting the table for supper. From the kitchen came sounds of frying and a girl's voice saying plaintively: "I'd no idea chips for twelve meant so many potatoes!"

Clearly there were enough people in the house —and ponies *around* the house—without Misty and me adding to their numbers for longer than one night. I'd find somewhere for Misty to graze. But it was hopeless. After ten fruitless telephone calls I realized that every inch of grazing in Marston-near-the-Sea was booked. The N.W. 17 Horse Club had moved in for the week, together with half the local riding school. There just wasn't a blade of grass that hadn't ponies and horses queueing to eat it; so there was only one thing to be done. Shushing Sally, June and Pete, who were greeting their newly arrived friends in the hall, I telephoned the vicarage.

Soon I heard Babs's voice at the other end of the line.

"Hello, Jackie!" she asked eagerly. "How did you get on? What time are you getting back?"

"I'm staying here to-night," I told her. "And I'll be bringing Misty with me by horse-box to-morrow." I tried to tell her what had happened, shouting to make myself heard above the noise from the Torrences and their friends in the hall. "So it's up to you," I told Babs. "You've simply got to find a field in Frensham where Misty can go to-morrow."

"I know just the place," Babs's voice came over the wire confidently. "It's not exactly a field. But there's grass, and Misty will like it. Or I *think* there is, and I *hope* she will. Anyway she'll have Captain for company. Goodbye."

"Hey, where is this grazing, and who—or what —is Captain?" I asked, but Babs had rung off.

I suppose she had flung down the receiver and rushed straight out of the New Vicarage to fix up about the field. It was no use ringing back. Babs would be half-way down Cedar Avenue by now. I'd just have to hope that Babs would have some luck.

With delicious smells of sausage and chips tantalizing me, and Pete and Sally yelling that my supper was going cold, I telephoned Mr

Brown, the local dealer, who, I knew, would be able to provide a horse-box to get Misty to Frensham next day.

CHAPTER FIVE

URGENTLY WANTED—GRAZING!

THE Torrences and their friends gave us a grand send off as Misty and I departed in Mr Brown's horse-box next day.

About two hours later I asked Mr. Brown to stop the horse-box half-way down Cedar Avenue near the New Vicarage gate to pick up Babs.

"Don't be disappointed about the grazing I've fixed up," Babs warned as she jumped into the back of the horse-box with Misty and me. "The field looks smaller than I thought, and I'm afraid there isn't much grass. Captain—he's a cart-horse friend of mine—hasn't been working lately because his master's in hospital, and I expect Captain's been consoling himself by grazing overtime."

My heart sank when we followed Babs's directions. We drove through a maze of town streets and at last pulled up in front of some iron railings which enclosed a small field.

30

As we stopped, a handsome brown-and-white horse—more cob than cart-horse—trotted to the railing and, sensing that there was a pony in the van, whinnied towards us.

"Well, at least you'll have company, my pony," I told Misty as we unboxed her.

But Misty was disappointed. I could see that she had expected a wonderful paddock, or an orchard like the one at Cherry Trees. Her hopes had been raised, and they fell as she lifted her head to the railings and looked at us in a forlorn way.

"Cheer up, Misty," I urged her. "I'll soon find you a better field. This is just temporary while I fix up something else."

"But how?" Babs asked. "There just isn't any-where else in Frensham, Jackie."

"I know," I told Babs. "But I've had an idea. Suppose I took Misty to Aunt Monica's farm at Newton Minster. She'd have lovely grazing there."

"She certainly would." I could see Babs was thinking about the rolling Downs and the good farmhouse and outbuildings, and the meadows sloping to the sand dunes and the English Channel. "Yes, it'd be super for her there, Jackie. Let's telephone Aunt Monica right away."

"After six o'clock," I said, "when the call will be at the cheap rate. Hiring that horse-box cost a lot more than I'd expected. With what your

31

mother might lend me I should just manage to pay for my board and lodgings, and stabling for Misty, when I ride her to Aunt Monica's."

"*Ride* her?" Babs echoed. "Aren't you going to take her in a horse-box?"

"I couldn't possibly afford to hire another horse-box," I patiently explained. "Besides, it's only fifty miles to Aunt Monica's. Misty and I could manage to ride twenty miles a day."

"You lucky thing!" Babs exclaimed. "I envy you. You'll have a lovely ride." Her face fell. "But Mummy will never agree to let you go."

"We'll see!" I said darkly, and for the moment I thrust that problem from me. "There are one or two other things to tackle first." I took Babs's arm. "Come on. We've got to find some hay for Misty. Will Captain's owner have any, do you think?"

"Jack Cooper? Didn't I tell you he's in hospital?" Babs reminded me. "Oh yes, I did, but I didn't tell you why. He strained himself, lifting boxes on and off the vegetable cart that Captain pulls. Well, Captain's a big friend of mine. I always gave him sugar when he came down Cedar Avenue." Babs looked thoughtful. "Let me see. Perhaps there's some in Mr Cooper's yard."

There was, so we gave Captain a feed as well as Misty.

"I'll call at the hospital to-morrow, and tell

Mr Cooper that we borrowed some of his hay," Babs said. "He'll probably be glad we've fed Captain. I think I'll come and feed him every day until Mr Cooper's better."

"*Quite* out of the question!" Aunt Alice said definitely when I tried to coax her to let me ride to Aunt Monica's. "A young girl of your age, riding all that way! I've never heard of such a thing! Your mother would think I was out of my mind if I let you go. Besides, Aunt Monica has quite enough to cope with on that farm of hers without having you and Misty wished on her."

I groaned. "But, what are we going to do about Misty? She's got to graze somewhere. Aunt Monica's farm is my only hope. And how am I going to get Misty there if I'm not allowed to ride her?"

Aunt Alice sighed heavily. She reached for the telephone, and asked the exchange for Aunt Monica's number at Newton Minster.

Soon she was explaining my predicament. I listened, trying to imagine Aunt Monica's re-actions as Aunt Alice said into the mouthpiece: "But, Monica, are you sure you can *cope* with Jackie and this pony? And what ought we to do? Suppose we both go halves for the hire of the horse-box? I mean, it's quite ridiculous for Jackie to ride *fifty miles*, staying goodness-knows where overnight."

B

Aunt Monica cut in then. I heard her voice come crackling over the telephone. And hurrah! She was all in favour of my riding to Newton Minster. You see, Aunt Monica is a very independent sort, and believes in young people tackling their own difficulties. She's also very downright, and I think she scoffed at Aunt Alice's wor-

ries. Then Aunt Monica apparently gave Aunt Alice chapter and verse of the route I was to take, and the name of a guest house where I might spend the first night and a farm for the second.

At last Aunt Alice put back the telephone.

"You and Aunt Monica win, Jackie," she said weakly. "But I don't like the idea. I don't like it at all!"

I hugged her. "I'll be all right!" I vowed. "I promise you! Oh, I'm lucky to have two aunts who are such good sports!"

"Count me out!" Aunt Alice said feelingly.

Next morning I said good-bye to Scamp and tried to make him understand that I'd see him again soon. Babs was going to put him on a through train to Newton Minster—labelled and in care of the guard.

Poor Scamp! He understood about my going away when he saw me getting my kit together. His stubby tail went down, and a sad look came into his brown eyes. He thought I was deserting him.

"Scamp, you darling, I love you," I told him. "And I promise we'll be together again very soon."

I pressed my cheek to his furry face and patted him. Then I said good-bye to Aunt Alice and Uncle James and went off to Cooper's field with Babs to collect Misty.

I strapped my rolled macintosh behind the saddle and with Babs's haversack on my back, swung myself up and set off. Misty seemed to sense adventure ahead. She sniffed the smoky air and stepped out briskly as though she knew she was on the way to country smells and soft grass under her hooves.

"Good luck!" Babs called, hurrying alongside as far as the corner.

Now there was just Misty and me, and the long road ahead, and hurrah! the sun was shining. I trotted Misty for a mile or so. Then I settled her to a long, steady walk until lunchtime. I found some juicy grass for the pony to graze. I loosened her girths while I sat under an oak tree to eat Aunt Alice's sandwiches and fruit cake. After Misty had rested for about an hour, I mounted again. I was loving every moment of the ride and so was Misty.

Sometimes she would give a contented snort and turn her head to look bright-eyed towards green pastures. When we stopped she nuzzled my shoulder and whickered gently. It seemed as though she realized that she and I were on our own—that we were setting out together on a wonderful adventure which would lead to a better life for her.

CHAPTER SIX

A SHOCK AT MIDNIGHT

I HEARD a clatter, and Misty slowed to an un-balanced walk. Yes, she'd cast a shoe. I should have to walk beside her, and find the nearest blacksmith.

The time was now four o'clock in the after-noon.

I walked with Misty a little way before we heard a bicycle rattle over a bumpy part of the lane behind us.

The rider dismounted. He was a carroty-haired, freckle-faced boy of about my own age.

"Hello!" he hailed. "Lost a shoe? I saw one in the lane a little way back."

I nodded and I told him briefly where I was heading and why.

"Congrats about winning such a super pony," he said in a friendly way. "But what rotten luck that there isn't a smithy nearer than Crosby Wood—four miles from here."

"Oh, goodness!" I groaned. "I'll never be there before the smithy shuts for the day."

"You haven't a hope." The boy thought, and then his face lit up. "I know. I'll bike on ahead. I know the blacksmith. His name's Weldon. He's a decent chap. He'll keep his forge going if I tell him you're on your way. By the way my name's Thorpe—Michael Thorpe."

I told him my name, and off the boy went, pedalling along the lane.

"We'll have to hurry," I told Misty. "Best foot forward."

At last we came to Crosby Wood which was a pretty village, with a pond on the green and a thatched smithy near a chestnut-tree. Michael was waiting outside the forge and there was an auburn-haired girl with him.

"Meet my sister, Angela," Michael said. "When I told her about your three-day ride, she simply had to meet you."

"We wondered if you'd stay with us for the night," Angela said, and I knew right away that she was every bit as friendly and helpful as her brother. "I've asked Mummy and she says 'Grand'."

"Thank you very much," I said gratefully.

"We've got a stable for Misty," Michael explained. "It hasn't been used for a long time. But it's clean and dry. There's a bed-sitting room above it—for the use of guests."

"It sounds lovely," I said.

"We'll get Misty some straw to sleep on and some oats and hay from the Harlows," Angela offered. "They're big friends of ours, and really keen show-jumpers."

I thanked the two Thorpes as I led Misty into the forge where Mr Weldon was waiting by the anvil.

Misty stood quietly while Mr. Weldon removed her remaining three shoes, trimmed her hooves and clamped on the new shoes.

When I paid Mr Weldon I felt glad that Uncle James and Aunt Alice had insisted on giving me an extra thirty shillings for what Aunt Alice called "Goodness knows what eventualities! And for heaven's sake, don't *squander* it, Jackie."

Well, a cast shoe was certainly an 'eventuality', and I thought gratefully of Aunt Alice when I broke into her pound note to pay the smith.

Waving good-bye to Mr Weldon, I set off with Misty and the two Thorpes. Their father was a country doctor, and his house and surgery were right on the village street. To the side of the long, low, brick front of the house was a cobbled yard and coach-house and stable with a guest room above. The coach-house was now a garage, and the stable was clean and comfortable as Michael had promised.

We'd only been there a moment when Angela's friends—the show-jumping Harlows—arrived and admired Misty. I half expected them to be too 'grand and know-all' for me, but they weren't. They were really keen about my pony-trek. Wendy Harlow said that Misty was a 'nice little mare' with good blood in her veins. We all became even more friendly after that. I *was* enjoying myself. The world and everyone in it seemed just wonderful.

Everyone was so eager to help. Wendy and her sister Mary went home and came back with a wheelbarrow and a bale of straw. Their older brother, Bob, turned up trundling another wheelbarrow behind him. In it were oats and hay. We rubbed Misty down, watered and fed her and made her comfortable. Then the Harlows went home, and Mike and Angela Thorpe took me indoors to meet their parents. Dr Thorpe was carrot-haired like Mike and had keen blue eyes in a kindly face. Mrs Thorpe was quite different —small and fair-haired, with a lovely smile.

After we'd all eaten a hearty tea Mike and Angela suggested tennis. I felt too stiff after the day's ride to join in, so I umpired until the light failed. Then we went indoors to supper and bed.

My bed-sitter was a pleasant chintzy room looking over the street, right away from the house, but I was too tired to feel lonely. The sheets smelled of lavender, and the bed felt cool and soft. I was too excited to sleep immediately. I lay gazing through the latticed window towards the full moon, half-hearing the voices and foot-steps of late-comers. I suppose I was just dozing off when I found myself listening to the steady clop of horse's hooves. The horse seemed to be walking. It came nearer. Who was riding so late? One of the pony-mad friends of the Thorpes?

Filled with curiosity I went to the window and looked towards the face of a girl I'd known all my life. Babs herself! Yes, Babs, astride a cob.

I rubbed my eyes to make sure I wasn't dreaming. But the girl *was* Babs, sure enough; and, as she rode nearer, I recognized her jeans and my blue sweater that she was wearing.

I saw that the horse was Captain—the green-grocer's cob, and that Babs was riding him in his harness bridle, with an old sack instead of a saddle.

41

"Babs!" I gasped as she passed below. She turned her head and saw me framed in the window. "What in the world are you doing here?"

"Looking for you," she said, quickly getting over her surprise at seeing me. "But I expected I'd have to track you down at the guest house at Tiverton where Aunt Monica said you might spend the first night."

"Why? What's happened?" I demanded.

"Something really dreadful," Babs said. "Or at least it would have happened if I hadn't acted quickly."

"What?" I almost shouted. "And how? Why? And where?"

"Not so loud!" Babs whispered. "Do you want me to be put in prison I've run away with Captain—to save his life."

"Oh, gosh!" I gasped.

Babs gently stroked the cob's glossy neck.

"The knacker was coming for him this afternoon," she told me. "There might be a hue and cry for him when he's found to be missing—and for me, too. Oh, Jackie, I do need your help—desperately—if we're going to save Captain!"

CHAPTER SEVEN

OUR DESPERATE SECRET

I LOOKED from Bab's worried face to Captain who, puzzled yet trusting, turned his kindly eyes to me as though he wanted me, too, to be his friend. I tried to think clearly. If Babs hadn't run away with Captain, then he would have been dead by now. Was that what she was telling me?

"You see, Jackie, Mr. Cooper *must* sell Captain," Babs went on.

"Why?" I asked.

"Well, he'd kept him as long as he could, but his green-grocery round was suffering," Babs explained. "The sad fact is that a horse isn't quick enough. Mr Cooper had to buy a lorry—or go out of business. He didn't *want* to sell Captain to the knacker, but he couldn't find any other buyer. Not many people want horses these days —not in towns, anyway."

"Poor Captain!" I leaned out of the window and saw the moonlight slanting on to the white blaze down the middle of his faithful face. "I suppose you found out all this when you went to the hospital to pay Mr Cooper for the hay," I said to Babs.

"Yes, Jackie. I sat by his bed for ages and *pleaded* with him," Babs said. "I told him I'd buy Captain myself—by instalments. Then the sister came into the ward and said time was up."

"So you went away and kidnapped Captain," I prompted, "to save his life."

"Yes, but, in a way, I hope I've *bought* him," Babs added. "You see, I left an envelope at the hospital for Mr Cooper, with five pounds fifty in it—all I'd got in my savings bank. I wrote a note promising to pay the rest in monthly instalments: thirty pounds altogether."

"But you don't know whether he'll accept?" I queried.

"No. And I daren't risk it. I think he's already made the deal with the knacker." Babs put out a hand and touched my arm. Her fingers were like icicles. "Help me, Jackie. You must!"

"Of course I'll help," I told her. "I think it's a rotten shame that a fine horse like Captain should have to be shot. But we can't go on talking here. We'll be waking the whole neighbourhood. Ride on through the village. I'll meet you at the cross-roads in about ten minutes."

I held my breath as Captain's hoof-beats echoed through the sleeping village. Surely somebody must waken and hear him. But I'd have to risk that. I dressed and made my way down the wooden steps to the stable. Luckily the bolts and the old-fashioned lock were well-oiled and I was able to let myself out noiselessly. I ran down the street to the cross-roads where Babs was waiting, with a tired and puzzled Captain.

Breathlessly I fired more questions at my cousin.

"Did you tell your mother and father about Captain? They love animals. They might have been able to help."

"I know, Jackie. But Daddy was at a ruri-decanal conference, and it was Mummy's day to help at the W.V.S." Her eyes glistened in the moonlight as the cob muzzled her shoulder at that moment. "Poor Captain would have been dead by the time they got home."

"But Aunt Alice and Uncle James must be out of their minds with worry, wondering where you are," I pointed out.

"I don't think they will be," said Babs. "I left a note saying that I was going to Aunt Monica's farm at Newton Minster to keep you company. And it wasn't really a fib, Jackie, because I *am* heading there. If *only* I can get Captain to Newton Minster, I'm sure we could persuade Aunt Monica to lend me the rest of the money to buy Captain."

"Yes, that's a possibility," I nodded.

"Captain's not an old horse. He's strong, with years of work in him."

"But the snag is, can we get Captain there before we're found out?" Babs said doubtfully. "We've got two days' riding ahead of us. We'd have to go by night, and—"

"Steady on, Babs," I urged, remembering her flair for being dramatic. "Why should we be furtive about this? Suppose we 'phone Aunt Monica now, and Aunt Alice too, and explain everything to them. Yes *and* to Mr Stephen Clarke. They'd all rally round, and I'm sure they'd save Captain somehow."

"They'd *want* to," agreed Babs. "But *could* they? There's only one *sure* way, Jackie. We've got to keep Captain hidden until Mr. Cooper agrees to give Captain a reprieve."

"Yes. You're right, Babs," I decided after a moment. "And we can't tell anyone else about this without putting them in a spot."

"Quite," Babs said. "Any grown-up would be in a terrific flap. They wouldn't want to betray Captain and us. On the other hand how could any grown-up agree to let me run off with a horse that didn't belong to me?"

I sighed. "Right you are, Babs," I told my cousin. "It's a wild scheme, but I'll back you up."

Captain snorted at that moment, and Babs hugged him and then me.

"Oh, Jackie!? You're a wonderful cousin to have. I knew you'd see it my way. Everything's going to be all right."

"I doubt it," I said realistically. I stepped into the road from the green verge and looked towards the moonlit village. "Stay here. I'll be back as soon as I can—with Misty."

I felt uneasy as I hurried to the Thorpes'. I crept to my room and packed my belongings. The Thorpes had been so kind to me, and here I was disappearing in the middle of the night without a word of thanks or explanation.

But wait—I could write something if I was careful what I said. I took my pen and wrote on the back of a chocolate wrapper which I found in my pocket.

Dear Angela and Michael,

I'm sorry to hurry away without seeing you, but I thought it best to make an early start and get Misty on the road before there's too much traffic about.

Please explain to your parents. Thank you all for your kindness. I do hope we meet again soon.
Sincerely,
Jackie Hope

But not too soon, I prayed as I put the note through the front door letter-box. I hated to mislead Angela and Mike, but I was hoping that they would jump to the conclusion that I had left soon after dawn instead of in the middle of the night.

I crept back to the stable.

Misty was surprised by my comings and goings. Poor old girl! The night must have seemed a short one to her. I fed her, saddled her, and rode her through the village to the cross-roads where my cousin was waiting for me.

Soon Captain and Babs, and Misty and I were riding through the open countryside together. There was something magical and wildly adventurous about it all. Something unreal and dreamlike. Maybe it was the silveriness of the moonlight, and the creak of pines in the night wind.

Misty and Captain stepped out well. They were glad of each other's company. Puzzled they might be—tired, too—but they loyally plodded on, doing their best for us as horses always will.

We did not want to ride them too far that night. Captain had already come a long way, and Misty had only had a short rest.

We let them drink deep at a stream. After that, they grazed on a triangle of grass by some cross-roads, and dozed while Babs and I made a pre-dawn breakfast of two slabs of chocolate— about half the emergency 'iron rations' that I had packed for the trip to sustain me between eating places.

Just before dawn we mounted and rode on.

A wind suddenly rustled over the countryside. Captain and Misty threw up their heads and cantered on the grass verge to the brow of the hill.

Moonlight was fading as morning's grey light appeared. Below us lay some flat meadows, low hedges, and the humped shape of hangars.

"This must be the old war-time aerodrome just outside Great Winton," I told Babs. "I wonder if it's used now."

There were no signs of sentries or guard dogs as we rode nearer. The aerodrome seemed quite deserted. The hangars were half-derelict. Even the barbed-wire and chain-link fencing had unrepaired gaps, and we could have ridden our mounts through at half a dozen places.

"Are you thinking what I'm thinking?" Babs asked.

"That this would make ideal day-time quarters for you and Captain?" I hazarded. "Let's see."

We rode to the nearest hangar. One of the side doors opened when we pushed. Inside was dim, dusty, but dry.

"You must be worn out, both of you," I told Babs as we led Captain and Misty into the hangar. "Here, take my mac, and lie down on it somewhere. I'll get some food from the village."

I had to wait until the village shop opened; then, my haversack bulging with bread, butter, cheese, bacon, tomatoes, and a bottle of milk, I rode back to the aerodrome.

Both Captain and Babs were sleeping, Captain on his feet and my wayward cousin curled up on my mac. They woke when they heard the rustle of paper as I unwrapped the food.

"Where am I?" Babs rubbed her eyes. "Oh, I remember now!" and she went over to make a fuss of Captain. "We'll need a fire to cook the food." She looked around her. "I suppose we'll have to light it in the hangar so that it won't be seen. Over there will do. The smoke should drift out through that broken window."

We collected dead wood from the hedgerows, and soon we had a fire going between two old bricks, and far enough away from any part of the building which might catch fire. Some of the smoke did go through the window, but most of it swirled round Captain, Misty and us in a weird sort of way.

Babs sandwiched slices of cheese between the bread, speared them on a stick and toasted them over the fire. They were delicious.

Then one of those fateful things happened— although one doesn't know they're fateful at the time! As I look back I seem to remember that I heard the chug-chug of a motor scooter, but since we were all under cover, hidden, I didn't think much of it.

A moment later the door of the hangar creaked on its hinges, and we spun round. Through the smoke I saw a youth of about seventeen, wearing goggles and a white crash helmet.

I blinked at him in dismay. Who was he? Was our secret to be discovered so quickly?

CHAPTER EIGHT

ESCAPE!

"HULLO!" the youth exclaimed blithely. "Where's the fire?"

"Right here," I replied, trying to sound friendly and carefree. By now I had managed to get over my surprise and I realized that Babs and I mustn't seem furtive, and thereby arouse the youth's suspicions. "We're cooking breakfast."

"Have some?" Babs invited, waving a piece of charred bread on the end of a stick.

"No thanks." He took off his helmet to reveal thick, fair hair. He pushed his goggles up on to his forehead. "I'm glad the place isn't on fire. I saw smoke coming through the window. So I thought I'd better investigate."

"Investigate?" I echoed blankly.

"Yes, I'm a reporter," the boy said. "My name's Robin Gosling. I scent a news story here."

"Reporter!" I echoed again and smiled modestly. "But no one would want to read about *us*."

52

"Two very young girls, two ponies, and breakfast in an aeroplane hangar certainly suggests news," Robin Gosling insisted. "Why, it might even hit the nationals—that is, be printed in the big newspapers—especially if you're a couple of runaways."

Behind Robin's back, Babs and I exchanged glances. We knew that Captain's life might depend on keeping our escapade out of the newspapers. Somehow we had to dodge Robin Gosling. Desperate measures were needed. I pulled myself together.

"How exciting!" I said, trying to sound as though I was pleased that the reporter was taking so much interest in us. I wanted to take him off his guard, so that somehow I might keep him in the hangar while we got Misty and Captain away. I gestured to the cheese and bread near the fire. "Toast yourself a cheese-dream, Robin, while we lead the ponies out of all this smoke before you ask us what you want to know."

A moment later, Babs and I had got Captain and Misty out of the hangar. From inside we heard Robin saying: "Gosh! The bread's come off the stick . . ."

We didn't wait to hear any more. We slammed the door, pushing the catch into position. I hooked through the metal loop the rusty padlock that hung on a chain from the door frame. We were just in time.

Robin crashed his shoulders against the solid door. The hinges groaned, but held.

"Let me out," he shouted through the door. "You can't do this to me. What's the game? You're up to no good!"

"Perhaps—though we haven't time to explain," I countered. "But we *are* sorry. Really we are!"

We mounted and broke into a canter as we left the tarmac.

Just before we reached the lane, I looked back towards the hangar. I didn't think it was possible for the young reporter to get through any of the windows. The frames were too small for him to wriggle through. All the same, we knew it would be only a matter of time— minutes, or at the most an hour or so—before he would be able to attract the attention of some passer-by in the lane.

"We've got to take cover quickly," I told my cousin. "I vote we make for Winton Forest over there. I expect there are lots of paths through it."

We rode through the forest for nearly an hour and a half, following one path after another. At first we tried to travel in an approximately straight line by riding into the sunlight.

Then clouds blotted out the sun, and we had only our instincts to guide us. I wished I had brought a compass on my pony-trek. Luckily, there had been a certain amount of forestry going on, so the paths were fairly clear. Of course, we had to keep on ducking to avoid the over-hanging branches. We rode on and on, following the winding paths through clearings, into hollows and up tree-clad slopes. Occasionally we had to jump trees that had fallen across the paths. At last we came to open fields. Had we

ridden right through the forest and come out on the other side?

We looked round and our delight turned to dismay as we realized that we had ridden in a circle.

We stared at the already familiar expanse of the Great Winton disused aerodrome below us.

The hangar door that we had fastened was swinging open. There was no sign of Robin Gosling's motor scooter where he had parked it near a gap in the wire. The young reporter was obviously again at large. Was he searching for us? Ought we to take cover?

"Never mind," advised Babs. "This is the last place he'd think of looking for us."

Just then I nearly jumped out of my skin as I heard a voice calling from behind me.

"Jackie! Thank goodness, we've found you at last!"

I breathed freely again as I realized it was a girl's voice, not Robin's. I looked round to see Angela Thorpe, and her brother, Michael, bumping along the path on their bicycles.

"We tracked you here," Angela told us. "Someone in the village said that you were seen riding off with a girl on a skewbald cob soon after midnight. We tried to read between the lines of the note that you left for us, and we scented a first-class mystery."

"So we decided to trail you, and we hope you don't mind," added Michael.

"Of course not," I said warmly.

"We saw smoke coming from the hangar window," added Angela, "and naturally we had to investigate."

"So it was you who let out Robin Gosling!" I exclaimed.

"Yes. How were we to know you'd locked him in for a purpose?" said Angela, laughing. "My word! He *was* annoyed."

"He tried to question us, but we didn't give anything away," added Michael. "In fact we sent him on a false trail—over by the Clay Alders."

"Oh, good. You *are* angels," I told them.

I introduced Babs and Captain, and explained the trouble we were in.

"Of course we'll help," Angela told Babs, obviously liking her at first sight. "That goes without saying. Now let me see—how can we get Captain safely to your Aunt Monica's?"

"You couldn't go more than a few miles without being discovered," Mike said thoughtfully. "Robin can throw out a terrific dragnet. Newspapers have correspondents in every town and village, and he could alert them to be on the look-out for you."

"Wait a minute!" We all turned to Angela who, by the tone of her voice, had been apparently struck by a good idea. "The Lester twins! They're good friends of ours. They're going to the County Show at Storminster in a few days, and they'll be taking two horse-boxes, so there's *bound* to be room in one of the horse-boxes for Captain and Misty."

"Yes, and that's on the way to your aunt's at Newton Minster," Mike explained.

"What a wonderful idea!" Babs exclaimed.

"But it means letting more people into our secret."

"You can trust Sybil and Frankie any time," Angela assured her. "Of course, we've got to take the risk of running into Robin Gosling between here and the Lester's. It's about two miles away. You could ride part of the way along the outskirts of the wood. Mike and I will go ahead on our bikes, and check that the route's clear. If we whistle two short blasts, that would mean danger. So take cover. Three long whistles will

mean the coast is clear."

We kept near the trees so that we could hide if need be. Was Robin, the reporter, still around? Or had he gone back to his office?

We soon knew the answer. A few moments later two whistles shrilled from round the bend. The danger signal!

Babs and I immediately put our mounts over a ditch and dismounted. We led Misty and Captain through some scrub until we were screened by the young oaks. We stood there tensely.

Five minutes later Babs broke the silence with an agonized whisper.

"It's the waiting that's so awful! ! What's happening? *Something,* of course. Otherwise Mike and Angela would have whistled the 'all-clear'. . . ." She broke off and her face became startled. "Listen! I can hear footsteps."

She gripped my arm. My heart pounded. Misty whinnied at that moment, and the footsteps broke into a run—in our direction!

One person might hide easily in the wood; two without much difficulty. But two girls *and* a cob *and* a pony! It was impossible. We just stood there, hoping a miracle would happen.

Then both of us began to giggle in relief.

The footsteps belonged to Mike and Angela.

"Thank goodness, it's only you two," I said. "Why ever didn't you give the all-clear?"

"We couldn't," Mike said soberly. "It would have brought the reporters hot on the trail. They might have seen all four of us."

"*They*—?" Babs prompted in dismay.

"Yes," Angela nodded. "It's Robin Gosling sure enough—complete with motor scooter and crash helmet. There's another youth, too, on a motor-bike. He's got a kind of leather box over his shoulder."

"A photographer!" I decided dismally.

Just then we heard the roar of a motor scooter and a motorbike engine, and then came a stillness as they cut off.

I turned to the others.

"I suppose they've left their bikes by the gate at the end of the meadow, and they're coming on foot," I said. "They'll track us by the hoofmarks. . . ."

"Sssh!" warned Babs.

"Hey, Geoff!" we heard Robin shout. "You cover that side and I'll search down here."

"Right you are!" replied the photographer.

"There's only one thing for it," I decided. "We'll have to split up, and meet at the Lester's place. What's the house called?"

"High Coppin, Shawbury," Mike said quickly. "Take the church's octagonal tower as your landmark, and you can't miss it."

I mounted, and turned Misty in the direction of the two youths' approaching footsteps.

"Don't try to stop me," I whispered not feeling as bold as I tried to sound. "See you all at High Coppin. I'm going to ride across Robin and Co's path to lure them from you and Captain, Babs."

"A decoy!" Babs murmured. "Gosh! You're game. Good luck!"

I touched Misty with my heels, and we sped round the oaks, through the scrub, and jumped the ditch. Misty rose like a bird. It was as though she was glad to be jumping again—jumping for joy.

I only wished I felt equally light-hearted.

"There's one of them!" Robin's voice rang out as Misty and I crashed into sight. "They must have split up. I thought they might. Stop her, man! Grab her reins!"

CHAPTER NINE

OUTWITTING THE ENEMY

THE photographer — a dark-haired youth — threw himself at Misty's head, but somehow he got entangled with his camera case. He missed, bounced against Misty's flanks and stumbled clear of her hooves.

My lips tightened. Now it was up to Robin. He was about twenty yards ahead, in the middle of the path. He stretched out his hands to bar my escape. He and his friend had evidently shut the gate behind them—perhaps to delay any break-through that we might attempt. The motor scooter and the motorbike were propped there ready to take up the chase.

I tugged at Misty's reins, and turned her head. We swung to the left a few feet from Robin's tense figure and outstretched arms. Over some stubble we cantered, with a pink-faced Robin running behind. I put the mare at some dense quickthorn.

"Please don't let there be any barbed wire," I murmured to myself. "Oh, please!"

There wasn't, and Misty sailed over the hedge to land comfortably on the grass. I waited there for a moment to give the youths a chance to take up the chase.

"Hey, come back!" shouted Robin. "What's the game? Hide and seek?" His voice, though raised to a shout, was now meant to be friendly. "Listen, I can help you, I'm sure I can . . . Where's the other girl and the cob? Well, at least stop and talk to a chap!"

"Not on your life!" I shouted.

I wheeled Misty round, and forced a challenging tone into my voice. I imagined Robin was just the kind of boy who would not be able to resist a dare. "Call yourself a reporter! You couldn't report an Old Folks' Treat! You and your motor scooter! You'll never catch me."

"Oh, won't I?" Robin retorted, sprinting towards his motor scooter at the gate.

"And as for that photographer of yours," I added loudly, "he's too sleepy to take a picture of a slow-motion snail."

That did it! The youth, whom Robin had called Geoff, started sprinting towards the gate, only a few paces behind Robin. I was fairly sure now that they would both chase me, and so be lured away from the spinney where Captain was hidden.

Then, when the coast was clear, Babs and Co. would be able to get away, and make their way to High Coppin, Shawbury, by some other route.

When Robin and the photographer were within a few paces of me, I put the gallant Misty at a hedge. She stumbled but recovered miraculously only to peck at she landed on the other side. So

I had been too clever, I thought, as I rolled over her head. I tried to fall in a relaxed way, and before I knew it I was on my feet again, mounting Misty and trotting her up the field.

The pony and I took our time now about our escape, going slowly to give the impression we were both winded. I didn't want Robin and Geoff to think it was hopeless to carry on the chase. That might make them decide to investigate the wood where Babs and Co. were still hidden. I looked back. They were astride their machines, putting on their crash helmets. They were talking rapidly as though they were deciding on some new plan. Both of them gave what sounded like confident laughs.

Then, sure enough, they set off on their machines. Good! I'd managed to lure them away from Babs and Captain, but what chance had I of escaping them?

And where was I heading? I didn't know this line of country. What lay beyond the crest of the hillside meadow? More woodland where I might take cover, or perhaps cornfields over which I couldn't ride? I soon knew. Below was the S bend of a river, with the octagonal church-tower of Shawbury on the other side. I realized that I was more likely to dodge the boys if I went straight ahead across the river.

Misty was tired, and I had hoped hard that I wouldn't have to put her at any more jumps. She'd had enough. She was even too weary to take any interest as some black-and-white heifers scattered skittishly when we rode down the other side of the meadow. I dismounted to open the gate that led to a main road.

No sooner had I shut it behind us than I heard

the dreaded chug-chug of the motorbikes. Robin and Geoff had already reached the riverside road. In another moment they would be round the bend and see me. I was a bit scared and quite worn out, but I wasn't beaten yet. Across the road was a gap in the stone wall, and a footpath that seemed to lead to the river. I rode Misty across the road and down the path.

I heard the youths give whoops of triumph as they saw us. I felt very young, all alone in the world, and ready to burst into tears! But I pulled myself together as frantically I glanced over my shoulder. Already they were rough-riding their machines down the path behind me. I galloped full-tilt down the slope. We reached the stony shore of the river. Misty whinnied with delight as she felt the cool water around her fetlocks. She dropped her head to drink. I jerked up the reins.

"Sorry, Misty," I murmured. "You may have a drink later. There isn't time now."

I could hear Robin and Geoff running to the water's edge, so I walked Misty into the deeper water. Soon she was up to her hocks. Then she swam and I shivered as the chilly river-water seeped through my clothes.

The force of the current caught Misty's flanks, and we went down-river sideways for a few yards. Misty didn't like this. She gave a startled whinny. Then her scrabbling hooves touched the riverbed and she waded to the bank. Meanwhile the youths were getting on their machines, having decided, I suppose, to cross the river by the bridge at the other end of the village. If only I could bluff them into giving up the chase! Perhaps I might make them think I was playing a game with them—a sort of catch-as-catch-can for the fun of the cross-country gallop.

"Well! Well! What fun!" I shouted to them across the river. I tried to sound light-hearted, when really I was at the end of my tether. "Thanks for joining me in a grand game of hide-and-seek!"

Quite distinctly I heard Geoff's reaction to my taunt. He turned to Robin, saying, "There! What did I tell you? There's no story, or picture. They're just a couple of silly kids, having a lark with us."

Robin murmured something I couldn't hear, and Geoff seemed to shrug. They sauntered back to their machines. Geoff had fallen for my ruse. But had Robin? Slowly, to give the youths the impression that I didn't care two hoots whether they followed me or not, I rode Misty along the bank for a few yards until I was hidden from sight by some willows.

The gardens of several quite big houses sloped down to the river, and, to my surprise, I saw, painted in white letters on a rustic gate, the house-name: HIGH COPPIN.

How odd! I should have thought a house with that name would be on a hill, or at least on high ground, not at the riverside. But who was I to quibble when my discovering the Lester house so quickly was such a super stroke of luck? The gate wasn't latched, so Misty was able to push it open with her nose. We walked along a garden path towards a wide drive. The house looked big and rather important, and I particularly noticed that there was a long range of stables.

The tall, thick cypresses that lined the drive also screened Misty and me from the road. I heard the noise of traffic, though—thank goodness!—nothing that sounded like the foreboding chug-chug of motorbikes.

Just then I noticed Misty's ears twitch, and a moment later I heard running footsteps on the gravel drive. Were Robin and Geoff still on the trail after all? I dismounted, and quickly led Misty behind a tall clump of laurel.

I parted the leaves to look out. The figure that sped round the bend was neither Robin nor Geoff. It was a girl. But what a strange-looking girl! I blinked and stared. She looked positively *weird!*

She was wearing a yellow cycle cape that ballooned round her bare legs. A bright, pink scarf was turbaned round her head, completely hiding her hair, and her eyes seemed to be blinking almost tearfully behind green-rimmed spectacles.

The girl certainly did look queer, and yet, as she got nearer, something about her features struck a familiar note.

She took off her spectacles to wipe her eyes, and I saw that the girl was weeping. Suddenly I gasped as she put away her handkerchief, and I got another glimpse of her face.

The girl was Babs!

CHAPTER TEN

SUSPENSE

"BABS! Why ever are you dressed like that?" I gasped. "And where's Captain? However did you get here so quickly without him? *And what's wrong?*"

"I'm supposed to be in disguise," she said breathlessly. "I had to alter my appearance in case I ran into Robin Gosling. I've rolled up the legs of my jeans, and Mike lent me his cycle cape. This is Angela's scarf." She touched her turban. "And her sun specs. Mike knocked out the lenses so that they'd look like ordinary specs."

I gazed at her and was about to laugh, but there was something about Bab's strangely woe-begone manner, her tear-filled eyes, and the wet clamminess of my own clothes, that made me cut short my mirth.

"I stopped a car, and begged a lift here." Her voice dropped. "I'm afraid I've got some bad news. It's Captain . . ."

She gulped, and paused.

"Go on," I said quietly.

"He's been taken ill. It happened soon after you'd ridden away. He sort of staggered and went weak at the knees. Mike and Angela are walking him up and down, trying to keep him awake. There's a purple stain on his mouth, and his bit's all frothy. I think he must have eaten something poisonous."

"Oh, poor Captain!" Like Babs, I was quite

numb with shock and dismay. "A vet! But, of course you've thought of that!"

"Yes, and luckily Mr. Lester's a vet," Babs explained. "I tried to telephone, but I couldn't get through. That's why I've rushed here."

I mounted Misty, and Babs ran alongside,

panting out the rest of the sad news as we hurried up the drive to High Coppin house.

"I've left Mike and Angela with Captain," she added. "Oh, Jackie, I feel so helpless. If only we knew what to do!"

"It seems to me that you did the sensible thing—hurrying to find a vet," I told her.

As she ran she took off the lensless specs, turban and cycling cape, and shook free her hair.

A moment later we came round the side of the house and saw two girls—obviously twins—with flaxen hair, and blue eyes. They were both be-jodhpured and wearing black velvet crash-caps. They were practising dressage routine in the paddock on two ponies that looked about as much alike as did the girls.

I blinked. It was as though we were seeing double.

I cantered up to the twin girls, with Babs only a few paces behind. We panted out the facts, not mentioning, of course, that Babs had borrowed Captain without the owner's permission, but explaining we were friends of Mike and Angela Thorpe.

"I'm Frankie Lester," said one of the twins, and I noticed she had a little brooch with an enamelled F inside it. "I'm sure Daddy will help. He's talking on the telephone now. He's been telephoning all morning about the arrangements for the County Show."

"That's why you couldn't get through," added Sybil who was wearing an S-brooch. "Go and tell Daddy, Frankie. I'll fix up Jackie with some dry clothes."

As soon as I had changed in the twins' bedroom, I hurried outside and joined Babs who was pacing up and down. I put my hand on her arm and tried to cheer her up, but my heart was as heavy as hers. Captain poisoned! What could be done to save him? There were a number of poisonous plants that Captain might have eaten while grazing. How on earth could Mr Lester know which antidote to use?

Then Mr Lester came out of the house. He nodded briskly to Babs and me and went into his surgery for his emergency kit, while Frankie led Misty into a spare loose-box.

We piled into the estate car, and sped down the drive. We were on our way now, and if anything could be done to save Captain, I felt sure Mr Lester would do it. But would we be in time?

When we got to the wood we saw Mike was holding open the field gate so that we could drive straight in.

"Please hurry!" he gasped to Mr Lester. "We couldn't keep Captain on his feet. He's lying down."

We rushed through the trees. Captain was on his side, amid the scrub. Angela was putting her folded blazer under his head, and was stroking

his neck. His breathing seemed slow and laboured.

I stared at Mr Lester, trying to read his thoughts. His face looked grim, and I guessed that he thought Captain was beyond help.

As we watched anxiously Mr Lester took a big hypodermic syringe from his kit, filled it and gave Captain an injection.

A little while later Captain's eyelids flickered only to close again. I stifled a groan. Suddenly Babs pressed my arm.

"Look!" she breathed.

I followed her gaze. A muscle twitched under Captain's satiny coat. A tremor ran down his back. His eyes half-opened. He seemed dazed. Mr Lester looked across at us.

"Now we must get him to his feet," he said. He took Captain's bridle. "Come on, old fellow," he urged. "Easy does it."

Captain stared blankly at the vet.

"Please try to get up, Captain," Babs coaxed.

Somehow the cob seemed to understand what we wanted him to do. He rolled on to his knees and tried to get to his feet. Angela, Frankie, Mike and I got behind his quarters and pushed while Mr Lester and Babs held his head. At last, with all of us either propping or holding him, Captain managed to stand squarely.

"I'm going to walk him up and down," Mr Lester told us. "You four—" he meant Babs and Mike and Angela and me—"stand two on each side, ready to steady him if he totters. Frankie and Sybil—" he turned to his twin daughters— "get out the Primus and brew some coffee. Captain's going to need a lot to pull him round."

For two hours we walked Captain along that leafy glade, stopping every fifteen minutes to force some of the strong black coffee down his throat.

At last Mr Lester said: "Now, we'll try to get him to our place. Frankie, hurry to the telephone box on the main road and tell your mother to bring the horse-box. Be sure to let her know exactly where we are."

Captain was allowed to stand still now while we all hovered round ready to act as props in case he showed any further sign of collapse. But he didn't. The pupils of his eyes were still quite small, but he did not seem nearly so dazed, and he managed to rub his muzzle against Babs's shoulder as though he realized all she had done to try to save him.

Quite soon Mrs Lester arrived in the horse-box. Captain, half-pushed, half-walking, went up the ramp. Babs, Frankie, Sybil and I climbed in with him and we were all on our way to High Coppin.

"I really think, in Captain's interests, that you two girls ought to stay with us for a few days," Mr Lester told Babs and me when he heard that we were on our way to Aunt Monica's. We could not tell him that he might be harbouring a wanted horse—only that we were on a pony-trek. "Captain will need careful nursing for some time, yet. He ought not to be left alone for twenty-four hours and after that he'll need rest or his heart may suffer permanent over-strain."

"We'll be very glad if you will be our guests, my dears," added Mrs Lester.

Of course we were overwhelmed with grati-tude. Mr and Mrs Lester were wonderful people and Frankie and Sybil were bricks. They took it in turns with Babs and me to sit with Captain in the loose-box. All that evening and through the night we watched over him. Twice Mr Lester came out to Captain—once to use the hypodermic syringe; once to give a drench: a long draught of the most horrible-looking medicine which Captain swallowed like the pet he was.

Toward morning Captain dozed and at seven o'clock Mr Lester came across to the loose-box to relieve Babs and me.

"I'll take over the next four hours," he told us. "You two girls go indoors and have some breakfast and a hot bath. Frankie and Sybil will take over from me at eleven. So you may have a morning in bed. Try to catch up on your sleep."

We thanked Mr Lester yet again for all he'd done. I felt almost light-hearted. Then, when I woke up hours later, a disturbing thought struck me. What about Robin and Geoff? I had forgotten them in the worry of Captain's illness, but now they came back into my mind as a danger to the cob's safety. Would they be on our trail again? I felt scared and rather on edge. Babs and I had told Sybil and Frankie about Captain and how we had tried to save him from falling into the knacker's hands. They promised to help us, and there and then we put our heads together to work out a plan that we hoped might make Robin and Geoff give up the chase once and for all.

So, after lunch I telephoned the county newspaper from a callbox and asked for Robin. Another reporter told me that he was 'out on a story'. What story? I wondered. Two girls—one

of them a clergyman's daughter—and a stolen
horse? I gulped, pulled myself together, and
asked to speak to a photographer named Geoff.
They put me through to another department,
and I soon heard Geoff's cheerful voice over the
line.

"Hullo, there!" I said. "I'm one of the girls
you tried to photograph yesterday. Your friend,
Robin, was trying to interview us. Remember?"

"I remember," he said suspiciously.

"Well, Babs and I wondered if you'd be free

for another cross-country event— motor bikes versus ponies. What about it? Where shall we meet?"

I wanted Geoff to think we hoped he and Robin would still trail us—that we had no story, but that we wanted them to join in another cross-country race.

"Meet?" he echoed indignantly. "We're too busy for kids' games. *Good*-bye."

There was an impatient click as he hung up. Babs and I and the twins hugged each other with glee after we'd left the telephone box. This was just what we wanted. Robin and Geoff apparently were not bothering about us.

Then we 'phoned Aunt Alice who seemed so overjoyed at hearing our voices that she forgot to be worried about us for the moment. She had jumped to the conclusion that we had already arrived at Aunt Monica's, and when we told her that, for a while, we were staying with a grand family called the Lesters, she fussed slightly and said she hoped we weren't being too much trouble. Luckily the 'pips' went before she had time to ask too many questions.

Next we telephoned Aunt Monica. We explained how Babs had joined me on the pony-trek, and that we had made some good friends on the way who had kindly invited us to stay for a few days, so that we could all go to the County Show at Storminster.

"Very well, darling," Aunt Monica said. "Take care of yourselves, and don't be a nuisance to those nice Lesters. Oh, hang on a moment. Here's someone who wants to speak to you."

A moment later I heard doggy panting over the telephone.

"Scamp!" I exclaimed. "So, you arrived safely!"

"Woof! Woof!"

I was thrilled to hear Scamp's barks again. Then Aunt Monica came back on the line to say he'd chewed part of the label tied to his collar. She had been there at the station to meet him, so everything had turned out well.

I felt on top of the world. But if only I could have foreseen what would befall us a few days later, I don't think I would have dared to be so light-hearted and carefree.

CHAPTER ELEVEN

AREN'T PONIES FUN?

LIFE was wonderful at the Lester's. The place was a pony-lovers' paradise.

Misty was given a good rest, grazing in the Lester paddock with the twins' outgrown ponies, Bumble and Dumpty. Captain had a roomy, airy loose-box in which to rest. Near him were the twins' show-jumpers: Rocket and Rusty, the chestnuts, who were actually brothers, which accounted for their looking so alike, and the greys, Moonlight and Moonbeam. All the ponies were just lovely, with intelligent heads, kindly eyes and lots of courage.

81

Frankie and Sybil let Babs and me ride the two greys for the first two days while Misty was resting. Then I rode Misty while Babs still kept to Moonbeam because Captain, although he seemed well enough in himself, needed a long convalescence.

We rode through the woods and over the Downs, jumping fallen trees and ditches. The twins were pleased with the way that Misty jumped. So, when Rusty strained a tendon, Frankie asked if she might enter Misty for the show in his place. I was thrilled! Here was Misty's chance to repeat past triumphs. Frankie gave her some schooling in the jumping paddock, and said that really she jumped quite as well as Rusty.

"Yes; she's a born jumper," Frankie said keenly. "Watch her over the triple bars."

My heart leapt as I saw Misty—the one-time firewood cart pony—canter confidently to the jump and extend herself over the wide spread. It was a big jump for a fourteen hand pony, but it didn't worry Misty. She was over with inches to spare, flicking her tail when she landed and eagerly pricking her ears as she looked for the next jump.

During our days with the Lesters everything was like a happy dream—so different from all the worry of the previous days. Of course we thought of Captain's owner, and Robin and

Geoff, but somehow they had drifted into the background. We began to think that perhaps there wasn't a hue and cry for Captain after all. Maybe Mr Cooper had been willing to take Babs's offer of paying for the cob on the instalment plan. Perhaps Robin and Geoff had decided there was no news story in our wild behaviour.

And our respective aunts and uncle didn't seem to be on the warpath.

Uncle James and Aunt Alice, at Frensham, and Aunt Monica, at her farm at Newton Minster, were even more delighted about Babs and me staying on at High Coppin after Mrs Lester had chatted affably with them on the telephone and said what 'nice, well-mannered' girls we were!

Mike and Angela Thorpe cycled over to the Lester's almost every day, and were thrilled that we were all having such a wonderful time.

Soon we were planning the arrangements for the show.

"Now let me see," Mr Lester looked thoughtfully at Babs and me after dinner one evening. "I think Captain will be quite well enough to travel on Thursday. So we'll put him in the second trailer with Misty. The showground is vaguely on the way to your aunt's farm at Newton Minster, so we'll take Captain with us and deliver him there before the show."

"Couldn't we keep him at the showground until it's all over?" Babs suggested, and I knew that she was wondering how Aunt Monica would take Captain's arrival. She didn't want to risk anything spoiling the fun of the show.

"Well, I don't see why not," Mr Lester agreed. "He'll be quite happy and comfortable in the horse-trailer. You might walk him around the showground for exercise. He'll probably thoroughly enjoy himself."

Babs and I were having a wonderful time among so many ponies. By day, we schooled and groomed them, and during the evening we read the twins' pony and horse books. There were story-books, show-jumpers' autobiographies, books on the care of the pony, on show-jumping seats, on mountain and moorland ponies, pony club annuals, and stacks of pony magazines. Babs and I were utterly happy, wallowing in the horse-and-pony atmosphere, and making enthusiastic plans for Misty's and Captain's futures.

"I'm going to ask for a saddle and bridle for a Christmas present," Babs planned. "Then I'll help on Aunt Monica's farm every holiday, and when Captain isn't working, I'll ride him. Perhaps I'll be able to make a jumper of him. After all, he won't be the first show-jumper that started life in a humble sort of way."

"Yes, plough horses and trap ponies—all kinds of horses have become famous jumpers," Sybil agreed encouragingly.

"And from what you tell me of how Captain jumped when you were escaping from that newspaper reporter and his friend, I should say Captain's got a natural flair," said Frankie, and then dried up because she remembered it had been decided that it was wiser for her parents *not* to know about our wilder escapades.

Meanwhile Misty's style was improving every day. She reined back in a supple way, flexed her neck and played with her bit when Frankie rode her round the paddock. She changed diagonals in her figures-of-eight as though she had been doing it most of her life—as she probably had, I decided, before the fateful accident that led to her pulling the firewood cart. But now she was to have another chance to win honours, and it was with great hopes that we boxed her in the trailer with Captain.

We camped overnight at the showground. Some friends of the Lesters had taken two horseboxes for two ponies, and at night they stabled both ponies in the one horse-box while the twins, Babs and I bedded down snugly, rolled in blankets in the second horse-box. The grown-ups, of course, were staying at the local hotel for the duration of the show, but we didn't envy them. Life in a horse trailer seemed quite perfect.

85

Cooking, for instance, was tremendous fun, and we all took it in turns to fry sausages and tomatoes, and to heat cocoa, on the two Primuses.

At last—the show!

The first class for the twins' age group was held at three o'clock on the first afternoon. Sybil had entered Rocket and Moonbeam, while Frankie was riding Moonlight and Misty. Sybil had two clear rounds, but Frankie took a toss on Moonlight at the in-and-out.

For a moment she lay quite still—stunned. Red Cross attendants ran across the ground towards her, and Mr Lester pushed through the crowd to get to her.

To everyone's relief, she staggered up and tried to remount, but Mr Lester was firm about not letting her carry on with the round. So it was rather a rebellious Frankie who led off Moonlight and told us sadly that her father had forbidden her to ride again that day.

"A touch of concussion!" she said bitterly. "Daddy's ordered me to lie down in the horsebox for the rest of the day. I suppose he's right. I must say I feel rather groggy. Sorry about Misty, Jackie."

"That's all right, Frankie," I said, trying to hide my disappointment.

"Why not give Jackie your competitor's number, Frankie?" suggested Sybil. "Let her ride Misty."

"Me?" I echoed weakly.

"Who else?" Frankie countered briskly. "Babs, be an angel, and tell the stewards. Hurry, Jackie! You'll be next in the ring. Here, borrow my black jacket and crash cap. Misty will take you round well enough. Just leave it to her. She knows her job!"

But did I know *my* job? Was *I* good enough? That was the question I kept asking myself as I rode Misty to the collecting ring. I'd never before jumped in a show, and some of the fences looked quite fearsome. Luckily I'd memorized the course by watching the other competitors, so I wouldn't be likely to spoil Misty's chances by putting her at the fences in the wrong order.

Leave Misty's mouth as free as possible, I told myself, and let her choose her own time for take-off.

"Come on, Misty!" I whispered to her as I mounted. "Show them all what you can do, and I'll try not to spoil things for you."

Now for it! Our number was called, and I cantered Misty into the ring. She knew what was expected of her, and she pricked her ears and went steadily at the first fence. She flicked her tail in delight as she cleared it and went on to the next. The clapping that followed was sweet in her ears. My! She *was* keen. Too keen? Was she going to rush her fences? Faster, she went. And faster! Would I be able to steady her without throwing her off her stride? With three clear fences behind her I fought to hold her back as she faced the fourth, a tricky stile. Five strides from the jump I let her go and she was up and over as though she had wings. Six more fences, and we had a clear round. Now for the jump-off with Sybil.

She had two ponies to ride, and had faults with both. Perhaps she was tiring from having already jumped two rounds. Or perhaps she was worrying about Frankie's concussion.

Misty won with a flourish. Flicking her tail in that joyous way which delighted everybody, she led the canter round the ring after she had received her rosette. No pony could have been happier. It was as though she understood that the good old days were back again. I made much of her, giving her slices of carrot, and gently stroking her ears in the way she loved.

"Hold it!"

I turned my head. There, camera-poised, was Geoff, Robin Gosling's colleague!

"Oh, hello!" I said doubtfully. "Did you manage to get a good picture?"

"I think so," he nodded. "I took some more of you while you were jumping."

"Did you?" I tried to be guarded.

"Yes, but of course you were too busy to notice." He put his camera in his case. "How's your cousin—the one with the cob?"

"How do you *know* she's my cousin?" I parried suspiciously.

I could see I wasn't going to get any reply except a disarming smile, so I asked: "By the way how's your friend, Robin Gosling?" And to make Geoff think that I had nothing to feel guilty about, I casually glanced round the showground, and added, "I can't see him here."

"Oh, Robin's fine!" He turned away and said over his shoulder, "You may not see him around, but believe me, like all good reporters, *he's still on the job!*"

I didn't like the sound of that. What were

Robin and Geoff up to now? Had Robin been making inquiries about Babs and me? Otherwise how would Geoff have known that Babs was my cousin?

Misty must have sensed my fears, because she thrust a comforting muzzle against my shoulder. Maybe Geoff was just trying to keep me in suspense and so pay me back in my own coin for the wild-goose chase I'd led him. I shrugged. I gave a carefree toss of my head, and walked away, deciding that I certainly wouldn't bother to tell Babs and the twins about Geoff's odd behaviour.

All the same I *was* worried.

It wasn't until I was back with the others, bedding down Captain and the ponies, making a camp-fire supper and discussing the triumphs of the day, that I really forgot my fears. At last we rolled ourselves in our blankets, talked sleepily, and felt glad that Frankie was now well again, without even the trace of a headache.

Babs switched off her torch, and sleepy 'sweet dreams' and 'let all your nightmares be ponies!' echoed through the horse-box.

I lay awake after the others had gone to sleep. Over and over again Geoff's foreboding words came back to me. He and Robin were plotting something. I was sure of it.

I suppose it was because I kept awake with that scared 'what's-going-to-happen-next?' feeling that I slept late next morning. I sat up with a jerk to find the horse-box open, and Mrs Lester standing with Babs, Sybil and Frankie, still in their pyjamas, all talking at once.

Suddenly I felt quite small and wished I could curl up and weep. The worst had happened. I was sure of it!

"It's all in the newspapers!" moaned Babs. "About us. You and me, Jackie. *And* Captain and Misty. We're in terrible trouble!"

CHAPTER TWELVE

OUR ESCAPADES EXPOSED!

"Oh, no!" I gasped. "How absolutely dreadful!"

"Now Jackie, dear," Mrs Lester said remarkably calmly, "please don't get upset. My husband and I want to help you—not to add to your difficulties. We understand that you and Babs must have acted through kindly motives because you wanted to save Captain."

"We'd have jolly well done the same!" Frankie said loyally.

"Only more so!" added Sybil. "I wish the reporters had interviewed me. I'd have told them a thing or two."

"You see, the story came out in the first edition of the *Daily Journal*," Frankie explained. "That's the national newspaper belonging to the same group as the County paper for which Robin and Geoff work. Apparently it's on sale in London soon after midnight. So all the other newspapers read about it and followed up the scoop. They've been telephoning half the horsey people in the County. At last they got on to

Daddy at the hotel, and one newspaper after another kept dragging him to the telephone."

"Naturally he didn't *tell* them anything!" said Mrs Lester. "But really he was dreadfully worried because, of course, he didn't *know* quite what you girls had been doing."

"And now that he does know," I gulped, "what does he think? That Babs and I are just a pair of silly young schoolgirls?"

"Well, I suppose he thinks what I think," she said in a weary voice: "That it's a pity you took the law into your own hands; it's really all a storm in a teacup, and it's a shame the newspapers haven't something more worth while to print than the—the . . ."

"The silly escapades of a couple of very young and very pony-mad girls," I ended for her. I held out a hand for the newspaper. "What does it say?" I asked in a small voice.

Babs's eyes looked at me in the way that Scamp's do when he's done wrong—spaniel-sorry!

"Oh, Jackie!" she said miserably. "I feel an absolute traitor. It was all my idea. I forced you into this, but it's *you* they've put in the headlines!"

My hand trembled. My throat felt dry.

"Let me see."

I blinked at the front page of the *Daily Journal*.

First I saw a photograph of Misty and me. It was the one which Geoff had taken when I had been patting Misty after winning the jumping competition. Then there was a picture of me on Misty as I took the gate at the show yesterday.

But the photograph that tore my heart was one I had never seen before. It was of Captain. He was shown pulling a grocery cart, and he was wearing a flower-decked straw hat with holes for his ears. He looked sweet.

This was an old photograph of Captain—perhaps a snapshot that Robin had borrowed from Mr Cooper.

Blushing with shame I looked from the photographs to the black headlines above the words:

EXCLUSIVE BY OUR COUNTY CORRESPONDENT
ROBIN GOSLING.
PONY PRIZE WINNER IN CROSS-COUNTRY ESCAPADE
SCHOOLGIRLS' BOLD BID TO SAVE GROCERY HORSE
FROM DEATH

Recent pony-prize winner in a nation-wide essay competition, sponsored by 'Horseshoes', a magazine for young pony fans, is Jackie Hope—the Girl with a Secret!

Yesterday when Jackie competed on her prize pony at a County Show, the on-lookers had not the slightest clue that she had—hidden in a horse-box nearby—a missing cob, Captain, for which the owner, and authorities, have been conducting a county-wide search.

One other girl shared Jackie's secret—her cousin, the daughter of a vicar!

Now the truth is out: that the two schoolgirls absconded with the hideaway horse, Captain, a grocery cart cob, and spirited him across country to save him from being humanely destroyed.

At the New Vicarage, Frensham, late last night, the Rev. James Maitland Spencer told our reporter: "Neither my niece nor my daughter informed me that they were kidnapping this horse. *Of course they acted entirely without my sanction. I had been led to believe that my niece, Jacqueline, was on a cross-country ride with Misty, the pony she won in the* Horseshoes *competition. It had not been possible to find any grazing whatever in the locality for the pony, and so Jacqueline was taking the mare to her aunt's at Newton Minster.*

"Later, my daughter, Barbara, joined her. Neither my wife nor I had the slightest idea that they had a missing horse in their possession, nor that the girls were camping out, and hiding the horse on an old aerodrome. This is all very disturbing news to me!"

There then followed some blah about Mummy and Daddy 'being distinguished archaeologists', and adding that 'until a late hour last night', they had not been able to be contacted by 'our Greece correspondent'. That was a mercy!

After that came an interview with Mr Jack Cooper, the Frensham greengrocer, saying that just as he was leaving hospital, he received Babs's note, together with some money: her 'first instalment' for Captain. There then followed Babs's note, and chapter-and-verse as to how Jack had already received thirty pounds from the knacker for Captain. Jack Cooper said he was parting with the cob with reluctance, but that he'd paid the thirty pounds to a garage as a down-payment on a greengrocery lorry. The only person in the town who was willing to buy Captain was the knacker.

Then there was a word with the knacker ruefully saying that—thanks to the vicar's daughter and me—he was now minus both thirty pounds *and* Captain!

At that point I had to turn to an inside page of the newspaper.

Page Five. The article seemed to go on and *on!* Goodness me! With all the really important things happening in the world, you'd wonder why the newspapers would want to write so much about Babs and me. I suppose they thought that a story about a couple of girls, a pony and a kidnapped horse might—if graphically pre-"sented—capture a nation's imagination. I suppose other newspapers also thought it was news value, because they too had printed the story and Babs was already poring over some of them.

The *Daily Journal* article by Robin Gosling ended by quoting from my prize-winning essay which *Horseshoes* had published—how I felt strongly that only young people who were level-headed and responsible should be allowed to own ponies and that no one should own a pony unless she or he had plenty of grazing available.

I groaned. There *had* been plenty of grazing at Cherry Trees. And I hadn't known when I'd written the essay that Mummy and Daddy would be setting off to Greece, and letting the house to the Torrences who would immediately *throng* the paddocks with enough ponies to account for every single blade of grass.

I crumpled the paper, and felt chokey in my throat. But before I could explode, I was showered with kindness from everybody around us. Mrs Lester was a brick. She told me that she'd already telephoned Uncle James to say that we

were safe and well, and that—no matter what the newspapers wrote—she was absolutely, *positively* certain that Babs and I had not done anything really terrible.

Babs and I then told Mrs Lester the whole truth, and I must say she took it all extremely calmly. She did say, however, that it was about time a grown-up took charge of the tricky situation to help sort out the shocking muddle.

Well, Babs and I had made such a mess of things that we were only too glad to find a grown-up who was ready to help. Firstly, Mrs Lester urged us to dress quickly. Then she took us to the hotel, and made us telephone Uncle James at Frensham, and Aunt Monica, at Newton Minster, to explain that we hadn't been *stealing* Captain, but only trying to save his life. Uncle James was slightly huffy about it all. But Aunt Monica seemed to be on our side right away. She said she could certainly make use of Captain on the farm, and that if he was sound in wind and limb it was a dreadful shame that he should be shot. For years, Aunt Monica said, she had felt it was a disgrace that lots of town horses were considered worth more money dead than alive. Furthermore she was going to write to the newspapers which had 'splashed' our story to tell them so. And she would *dare* them to put it in big print, too.

And, added Aunt Monica, in her most downright manner, she wasn't ashamed to have two nieces who had such spirit and if she'd have been in our shoes she would have done the same. That wasn't all: when we arrived at Newton Minster, she'd give us, Misty and Captain, the welcome we all deserved—and the holiday of our lives!

"There go the pips," ended Aunt Monica briskly. "See you soon!"

"Hurrah for Aunt Monica!" Babs exclaimed. "I never knew grown-ups could be so sensible!"

Our spirits were still soaring as we hurried back with the twins to the trailers. We let out Misty and Captain and walked them round and gave them their feed.

"You don't have to be a 'hideaway horse' any more, Captain," Babs told the cob, stroking his smooth neck. "You're going to a lovely farm, and you'll never have to go back to smoky graz-

ing and town streets again. You'll work with other fine horses, and when you grow old and tired you'll doze your days away in a shady pasture—" She broke off. "I suppose, everything *is* all right," she added doubtfully, turning to me. "I mean the knacker or Jack Cooper, or whoever *owns* Captain, would be willing to sell him to Aunt Monica."

"I'm sure he would," I said. "Jack Cooper wouldn't have let the knacker have Captain in the first place if he'd thought he could have found a ready buyer for him *alive*. And if the knacker wants to make a profit on the deal, Aunt Monica won't quibble."

"Yes, we can safely leave it to Aunt Monica," Babs nodded. "She's more than a match for any of them."

As you've probably guessed, Aunt Monica is quite an unusual sort of aunt. She held a high rank in the Land Army during the War, never married—she'd always said she'd never met a man yet who wasn't scared of her. Yes, sometimes she could be rather frightening, but everyone really loved her.

"She's a poppet," Babs decided. "Now if I'd had you with me to advise me, Jackie," she added thoughtfully, "and if there hadn't been need for *haste* to save Captain, maybe I would have enlisted Aunt Monica's help before I kidnapped him."

"It's easy to be wise after the event," I consoled. "Anyway, everything is more than O.K. now."

Yes, a world of ponies, horses, shows and *real* people like the Lesters and Aunt Monica, was a truly wonderful place.

"Now what next?" I wondered aloud.

"Breakfast!" The twins said in unison, and

only then did Babs and I realize how hungry we were.

Frankie looked at her watch.

"We'll have to hustle to get the ponies ready for today's jumping," she told us.

So about an hour late, Misty and I were in the collecting ring waiting for our class. Frankie, Sybil and Babs were elsewhere, grooming the other ponies. Just then the sun went behind a cloud. I happened to look up and saw a blue coupé drive into the parking ground. I could read the black, block letters of a label on the windscreen. On it was the one dread word: PRESS.

I glared indignantly.

Then out of the car stepped the last person that I expected to see: Mr. Stephen Clarke, editor of *Horseshoes!*

CHAPTER THIRTEEN

A FATEFUL DECISION

I GROANED as I noticed that Mr Clarke had a sheaf of newspapers under one arm, and that the expression on his usually cheerful features was strangely serious. He glanced round the showground as though he were looking for someone. He caught sight of me, and I knew, by the way his eyes flickered, that I was the person he'd come to see. I walked Misty across the collecting ring towards him as he ducked under the rope.

"Hello, Mr Clarke," I said, trying to give a bright smile.

He gazed at me sorrowfully, and then he shifted his feet as though he had a nasty job to do.

"Yes, and I'm afraid I've bad news for you,
103

Jackie." He spoke quietly. "I've been sent down from London by my directors to talk to you. They called a meeting early this morning, and passed a resolution—"

"Yes," I said in a small voice. "Go on."

"They feel that *Horseshoes* ought never to have awarded a pony prize, because of the risk of the pony getting into wrong hands. In fact, they think that is what has happened, Jackie—partly because of the publicity in the newspapers, and the fact that you had no grazing for the pony after all . . ."

"I *had* when I wrote the essay," I pointed out, and suddenly I felt very indignant. "I *won* Misty. She's my pony. No one can make me give her up. Besides, she will get good grazing. She's going to stay at my Aunt Monica's farm until Mummy and Daddy come back from Greece, and the Torrences move out of Cherry Trees."

Mr Clarke sighed.

"Believe me, Jackie," he assured me. "I'm on your side. I fought to stop the directors passing the resolution. But the national publicity had made them very angry. They were all against our giving a pony as a prize in the first place. They wanted to give money instead. They foreshadowed the difficulties of awarding the pony prize to someone who might not be able to offer it a good home. I persuaded them that those difficulties could be overcome by making it an essay competition so that the judges would learn the reasons for wanting a pony, and whether the winner would be able to keep it properly. Do you follow me?"

"Yes, and I promise you I can do right by Misty. Why, this show proves it. We came in first in the Under Fourteens yesterday, and in a few more minutes we're in the Open. You'll see how well Misty's been jumping for me." I saw Misty's ears flicker as she heard her name mentioned. "She loves me. You can't take her away. I won her fairly. I didn't write any lies."

"Look, Jackie—you'd still get a prize—a money prize," Mr Clarke tried again, looking even unhappier than before. "We'd make sure that Misty was sold to a good home, for a fair price, and you'd have the money, of course."

"I don't *want* the money," I protested, trying not to sound tearful. "I want Misty." Misty was pulling away, straining towards the jumping ring, eager for the competition to begin. "I won Misty fairly and I'm going to keep her!"

Mr Clarke turned away. His shoulders sagged. He looked worried. I felt terribly guilty. I called him back. There was something I had to know.

"Will you get into trouble with the directors, Mr Clarke, when you tell them I'm going to keep Misty?" I asked him bluntly.

He hesitated before he said, "I was made editor of *Horseshoes* on six months' trial. The trial period ends next month. The directors have told me bluntly that they won't renew my contract if I can't get you to agree to give up Misty."

"I suppose they're scared that their giving a pony prize to such an unsuitable girl as myself will harm the magazine," I retorted. "I think they're quite wrong".

"So do I," Mr Clarke agreed quietly.

"But the fact remains," I pointed out, "that either I give up Misty or you lose your job."

Mr Clarke nodded. I looked at Misty and then dragged my gaze away from her. She would be just as happy—and as well-cared-for—by some other girl. Of course I knew that. Misty had grown fond of me during the few days she'd been mine. She was a friendly, affectionate pony. She'd fret for me; then, after a while, she'd forget. She'd be just as keen to do her best for some other girl; she'd be loyal and faithful to someone else . . .

But I'd never forget her—not in a life-time of horses and ponies. There'd never be another pony like Misty.

Suppose I insisted on keeping Misty? Would I ever forgive myself for being the cause of Mr Clarke's losing his job after he'd been so kind to me? He sighed heavily just then, and I knew there was only one thing to do—let Misty go to a good home.

"Fair enough!" I was heart-broken, of course,

but I was trying not to let Mr Clarke see it. "I'll give up Misty if you'll guarantee her a good home, and I'll take the money as the essay prize."

"Very well, Jackie," said Mr Clarke. "I'll try to find a buyer for Misty right away."

Just then I heard my number over the loudspeaker. I was being called into the ring. I mounted Misty, and rode away from Mr Clarke. As we went into the ring I heard the commentator give my name, and Misty's name, and add something about Misty being a prize pony, and that we had both done well yesterday, and had also hit the headlines this morning. His remarks were meant good-naturedly, and so was the amused ripple of laughter that came from the onlookers.

If it hadn't been for that laughter, I might have been able to control myself. The laughter was *happy*—and somehow it touched off the utter sadness inside me. I felt the tears rush to my eyes. Sobs were choking in my throat as Misty cleared the first rails. I fought to stop the tears rolling down my cheeks. They welled up, blinding me. I couldn't see!

I tried to brush them aside, hoping people would think I'd got dust in my eyes. Misty slackened her pace and turned her head to me as though wondering why I was not in control. The tears cleared, and I put her at the next jump.

She sailed over joyously. I heard the commentator's voice over the loudspeaker.

"I've just been handed a note saying that the pony now in the ring, Misty, owned by Miss Jackie Hope, is for sale. So if there is anyone who would like to own a fine-jumping mare—a prize pony and a potential cup winner—now's his—or her!—chance."

As I listened I realized Mr Clarke must have had the announcement made, feeling that he was doing his best for me by trying to find an owner quickly.

Now it was quite impossible to keep back the tears. They filled my eyes, and I couldn't see a thing. So I had to let Misty take charge while I rode blind. Over one jump she went: then another. At one point she paused, waiting for the aids that I was not able to give because all I could see was a tearful blur. Again she jumped and again, clearing jump after jump. I heard a gasp go up from the crowd, and didn't know why until—with a whinny of triumph—Misty cantered from the ring, and I heard the commentator say over the loudspeaker: "I'm not sure quite what went wrong there. Misty jumped magnificently, but the rider—Miss Jackie Hope —unfortunately put her at the jumps in the wrong order. She is, therefore, disqualified."

What did it matter? I patted Misty, giving her all the lumps of sugar that I had in my pockets. I wiped away my tears and blew my nose vigorously.

I felt someone touch my arm, and turned to see a girl of about my own age. She'd been in the Under Fourteens yesterday and she'd come in fourth.

"Is this pony really for sale?" she asked me.

I nodded. "Yes. She is."

"Well, I think Daddy might like to buy her for my brother," she told me.

"Oh, yes?" I tried to smile. I must pull myself together if I was to do my best by Misty. "I hope you don't mind my asking, but have you got plenty of grazing?"

"Yes, two paddocks," she assured me. "I can promise you Misty will get a good home. We're all horsey people in our family." She brought a stub of a pencil and an old envelope out of her pocket. "Look, I'll write down my name and address, and draw a map, so that you'll be able to find our place."

I blinked at the piece of paper that the girl had given me. She was named Banting. *Valerie* Banting. I remembered the Bantings' house. It was a rambling Victorian place with the rather important-sounding name of Charnwood St

George. Sybil Lester had pointed it out to me when I'd ridden beside her in the horse-box to the showground. I recalled noticing the wonderful paddocks and wide parkland with white-painted railings.

I tried to tell myself that I was lucky to find such a wonderful home for Misty. I thought I'd better get the parting over at once before I'd time to think too much about it.

"I'd like to ride Misty over to your place right away," I told Valerie Banting. "Will you father and brother be there this morning?"

"Well, they're *bound* to be there at meal-times," Valerie said. "That's a good idea! If you started now, you'd get there for luncheon, and you could eat with them. I'll telephone them so that they'll expect you."

As I led Misty from the showground, Babs, Sybil and Frankie came hurrying out of the refreshment tent. They were frantically looking around—for me!

When they saw me they made a combined charge, firing questions.

"That announcement!" Babs exclaimed. "It must be a mistake. You can't be going to sell Misty."

"Yes, I am," I said and explained what had happened. "It's the only way. I'm going to take Misty to her new home right away."

CHAPTER FOURTEEN

MISTY TO THE RESCUE

BABS was upset. She tried to say something but
choked.

I turned and swung Misty on to the grass by
the roadside. I cantered for a little way; then I
put her at a low hedge and rode along a path
over a meadow, taking the cross-country route
to Charnwood St George—the route that Valerie
Banting had drawn on her rough map.

The noise of the show ring was behind us.
Misty and I could still hear the pounding of
hooves between the jumps, the ripple of ap-
plause, the voice from the loudspeaker, calling
the next hopeful competitor into the ring.
Misty's cat-like ears twitched as she heard it all,
and half-turned her head as though she wanted
to be back there again, showing how well she
too could jump.

I soothingly stroked her neck. Our last ride
together. . . . I knew I'd remember every moment of it for the rest of my life. I noticed the

gentle curve of her neck; I thought of her eagerness to please and obey, and her utter trust in me.

"I'm not letting you down, Misty," I whispered. "Honestly I'm not. I'd never sell you just for profit—not for a million pounds. And I don't think I'll ever love another pony as much as I love you. The way I feel now, Misty, I'll never want to own a pony again."

That's how much I cared for Misty. I felt that if I couldn't keep Misty, I didn't want any other pony—ever!

A breeze blew up, rippling her mane. She threw up her head as though to let me know she was fit and happy and ready to gallop. She went flat out for about a quarter of a mile along a river bank. I pulled up to take my bearings. Yes, there was the fir copse on higher ground. Valerie had told me that, when I reached the copse, I'd see Charnwood St George sprawling on the plain below.

I pictured it in my mind's eye long before I'd reached the higher ground. Misty's future home: wide, green, juicy acres—everything a pony could want. Other ponies for company. Owners who loved and understood animals. Everything was there for Misty—except me. But ponies soon forget, and Misty's loving heart would find happiness in giving affection and loyal service to Valerie and her brother.

Yet it's almost always the unexpected that

happens. Odd, isn't it? All I expected to see below me, from the hill, was the Banting's house. I did see that. But what I also saw was so surprising that I caught my breath. I gazed down at the road below, and suddenly felt very angry.

About twenty yards away, quite unaware that I was watching them, were Robin Gosling, the reporter, and his photographer friend, Geoff. They were at the side of the road, and Geoff was trying to light his pipe, using a lot of matches as beginner pipe smokers always seem to do. They were joking together as though they hadn't a care in the world. Then when Geoff had got his pipe well lit, he hitched his camera-case over his shoulder. I noticed that neither of them was wearing crash helmets this time. Robin mounted his motor scooter, and Geoff got on the carrier.

Perhaps Geoff's motor bike was being repaired, and Robin was giving Geoff a lift, and they'd stopped so that Geoff could light that pipe of his. I suppose they were on their way to cover some story or event together.

The motor scooter wobbled as they set off. The youths laughed and disappeared round the bend.

Next moment they came into sight again as they rounded a bend lower down the hill. They must have struck a rut in the road because they wobbled badly again. They laughed, but oddly nervously this time. They dipped out of sight.

Then — immediately — I heard a crash that sickened me.

There was a terrifying silence. No laughter; no voices; no chug of the motor scooter. Just— *nothing* until Misty gave a startled whinny, and shivered violently.

I galloped Misty to higher ground where I

could see what had happened. The motor scooter was on its side with the front wheel buckled, near a telegraph pole. Robin lay in a crumpled heap a yard or so away, and Geoff was in a squatting position, holding his head in his hands.

A flow of liquid trickled from the petrol tank. And that wasn't all. Geoff's pipe had been flung from his mouth. It was on the verge, and the glowing ashes had set fire to the dry grass.

Robin and Geoff were in more danger than they realized. Any moment now that flow of petrol might reach the burning grass. There would be a flash—and a blazing fire, all around the youths. I shouted to warn them, but I th'nk they must have been too shocked and dazed to hear. Meanwhile I'd instinctively urged Misty forward. We sailed over a land-drain, and galloped across some stubble. A hedge lay in our path, but we were over that, and over the ditch on the other side.

Misty slid down a steep, stony slope, and suddenly came upon a solid, five-feet high, dry-stone wall. I glanced towards the scene of the crash. The trickle of petrol was a gush now. A breeze was fanning the blazing grass, carrying the flames to meet the flow of petrol. It would now be only a matter of minutes before the flames would set fire to the petrol.

"Go on, Misty, *please*!" I begged. "You can do it! I know you can."

I dreaded that she would refuse the wall. No one could have blamed her. But gamely she tackled it, almost from a standing jump. I helped her all I could, but I was afraid that she might fall and hurt herself.

By some miracle, she was over. She stumbled in the road, quickly recovered, and raced to the crash. I jumped off her back.

"Geoff! Robin!" I shouted, almost out of breath. "Fire danger! Get clear!"

Geoff dazedly raised his head, but his eyes looked blank. I put my hand under one of his arms, trying to get him to his feet.

"Fire!" I shouted near to his ear, and pushed him clear.

I turned to Robin. He wasn't unconscious. He was writhing on the ground, clutching his middle as though badly winded. Still shouting 'fire danger,' I grabbed the leather shoulders of his wind-cheater and tugged. He was heavy, but I managed to move him nearly a yard. Then there was a blinding flash, and intense heat and flames all round us. I found that Geoff was now standing unsteadily beside me. He'd recovered enough to help. Together, we dragged Robin clear of the fire. I ripped off my smouldering jacket, and used it to smother the flames that were dancing on Robin's clothes.

The motor scooter was rapidly burning out. Meanwhile, terrified by the sudden flash, and my warning shouts, Misty was in the middle of the road, rearing, rolling her eyes and squealing with terror.

Just then part of the burning motor scooter exploded with a sharp report. Misty bolted up the road. I quickly looked at the two still-dazed youths, and myself, to check that our clothes were no longer burning, and I ran helter-skelter after her.

"Misty!" I shouted. "There's nothing to be scared of. Come back, Misty!"

She was out of sight, round the bend. I heard her hoof-beats slacken, and then stop. Sure enough, she was standing, trembling, near to the hedge, fighting her fright. I soothed her until she was calm before I led her back to the scene of her scare.

Geoff and Robin, both trying not to stagger, were coming down the road to meet us. Black smoke curling from the wreckage of the motor scooter meant, I suppose, that the petrol had burnt itself out. The two boys helped me to lead Misty away from the choking smoke. We all sat on the grass bank, getting back our breath.

Geoff was the first to speak.

"Phew! What a narrow escape! If it hadn't been for you and Misty, we'd have been burnt to a cinder."

"Rot!" I retorted briskly because I was still so angry with the youths that I did not want their thanks. "You'd have crawled clear."

"Not a hope!" Robin exclaimed. "I was so winded that I couldn't even stagger to my feet."

"And my head was spinning so much that I couldn't see or think straight!" Geoff said, gingerly touching a bruise on his forehead. "I didn't even *know* there was any fire risk. And I wouldn't have known it until we'd gone up in flames."

"So thanks a lot, Jackie," Robin said. "You're a heroine!" He smiled at me. "And, by golly, you deserve to be in the headlines again. My motor scooter's gone up in smoke, but it's insured, and we've got a scoop right here. So none of us need feel down-hearted."

"I think you've done quite enough scooping," I said coldly. "And if you feel that any thanks are called for, spare some for Misty." I pointed to the high ground beyond the stone wall, quickthorn hedge and land-drain. "Misty and I were away up there about half a minute before the crash."

They gazed to where I pointed.

"You mean to say that you and Misty jumped that wall to come to our rescue" Robin staggered up and flung his arms round Misty's neck. "Misty, you angel, I'll keep you supplied in sugar for the next five years." He looked back at me. "And your mistress in chocolates—if she'll let me."

"Thanks," I said coldly. "But all I want is that you both stay out of mine and Misty's lives for ever. I hope I never see either of you again!"

CHAPTER FIFTEEN

MORE HEADLINES

BOTH boys seemed completely flabbergasted by my outburst.

"Hey, steady on!" Robin protested, stepping back and staring at me as if he couldn't believe his ears.

"Maybe you didn't realize what harm that story would do," I told them. "But the result is that I've got to give up Misty."

"I don't get it," Geoff broke in. "Robin wrote that news story in such a way as to *help* you save Captain's life. What went wrong?"

Quickly, I explained exactly what had happened that morning; the unexpected arrival of Mr Stephen Clarke at the showground, and how his directors had told him to get me to agree to give up Misty. As Robin and Geoff listened I could see that they were sorry about what had happened. Truly sorry. But that didn't help either me—or Misty.

"But those directors *can't* do this to you!" Robin exploded.

"No, but they can sack Mr Clarke if I don't do as they say," I pointed out.

"It's unethical; it's unfair; it's undemocratic!" Robin couldn't have been more indignant, but, at the moment, this wasn't much comfort to me. "They must be off their rockers. Don't they realize that the publicity we gave *Horseshoes* is worth hundreds of pounds; that it'll put up their circulation by a thousand or more?" He looked straight at me. "Honestly, Jackie, if it's the last thing Geoff and I do, we'll see that you and Misty don't part."

I wanted to weep. If they'd both been older brothers of mine, they couldn't have been more keen to make amends.

Yet the harm was done, and what could these two youths do to influence those pig-headed directors? I supposed I'd have to forgive Robin and Geoff. They'd only been doing their job. And how could they possibly have guessed that the directors of *Horseshoes* would panic about the publicity?

"Listen, Jackie," Robin began in his most big-brotherly way. "We've got to help you out of this mess, and this is what I suggest. Suppose

I write a news story something like this for all editions of to-morrow's *Daily Journal.*" Robin's eyes lit up: *"The editor and directors of* Horse-shoes, *that leading and favourite journal for horse- and pony-lovers of all ages, are to be congratulated in picking two worthy winners: Miss Jackie Hope, and her grey Welsh mare prize-pony Misty.*

"For, yesterday, this gallant rider and pony saved two young men from being seriously burned. To drag the victims of a motor scooter crash away from the burning machine, Miss Jackie Hope set her pony in a wild race against time. Over ditches, a hedge and high stone wall, they jumped, arriving just in time to pull the dazed victims clear—"

I put my hands over my ears. "Please shut up!" I insisted inelegantly. "You do talk the most awful rot."

"But it's the truth," Geoff added. "No more: no less."

"And the news editor of the *Daily Journal* will wear it. I mean he'll print it more or less in that wording, if I explain all the angles," Robin said definitely. "I'll suggest that he also has a personal word with the manager of *Horseshoes.* For instance, he might congratulate the directors on having such a good editor as Mr Stephen Clarke. He could convince the directors what a circulation-booster the *Daily Journal* publicity really is. Furthermore, he could offer Mr Clarke a better job on the *Daily Journal*."

"But would he?" I doubted.

"Would he not?" Robin echoed. "The *Daily Journal* group of newspapers and magazines is simply crying out for skilled editorial staff. How would that do?"

"But suppose Mr Clarke didn't want to leave *Horseshoes*," I pointed out.

"Then it's on the cards that his directors would change their minds and let him keep his job. Yes, and probably with a rise in salary, too."

"And if they do that, I'd never have to part with Misty," I said. "All right. Print it!" I mounted Misty. "Now I'll have to find a telephone and let Valerie Banting's people know that I won't be arriving for lunch, and that maybe Misty won't be for sale after all. I'll be at my aunt's by midday to-morrow. 'Phone me there, Robin."

In next morning's *Daily Journal*, the news story and photos of Misty and I were splashed over the front page—just as the two boys had planned.

But it was not until the middle of the afternoon that Robin telephoned me at Aunt Monica's farm to tell me the outcome.

I listened to what he had to say. Then I ran to

tell Babs. I couldn't find her. She was out somewhere with Scamp. I had to tell someone, so I ran to Misty's paddock. She whinnied as usual when she heard me coming.

I flung my arms round her neck and pressed my cheek against her. It was feeble of me. But I wept. I couldn't help it. I howled! And then I stopped because I could see I was upsetting poor Misty.

A mournful look had come into her eyes, and she was thrusting her nose against my shoulder to try and comfort me.

"It's all right, Misty," I told her. "I'm not sad. Nothing's wrong. We're not going to be parted. The directors of *Horseshoes* are letting Mr

Clarke keep his job, and they don't want me to sell you after all."

Misty gave me such a powerful nudge with her muzzle at this point that I almost over-balanced.

"You're always going to be my pony," I said. "Don't you understand, Misty? You're mine for keeps!"

That night Babs and I were safely and snugly in our bedroom under the eaves at Aunt Monica's farm. The moonlight made the night quite magical. It was slanting through the dormer window on to Scamp who was curled up in the corner. Out there in the paddock Captain and Misty dozed peacefully. I could see them from my pillow.

"Happy dreams," I murmured to Babs.

But she was already asleep, I made myself keep awake for a little while. I wanted to think about all the good friends we'd made since Misty and I had set off from the New Vicarage.

Goodness knows what Babs and I had done to deserve that things should turn out so happily for us. We'd been wayward, impulsive—and taken the law into our own hands. We'd done something which certainly wasn't a pattern of good behaviour for other pony-mad boys and girls. We realized that only too well.

But at least we'd tried to deserve the friendship, service and loyalty that horses and ponies give so unfailingly.

Ponies, dogs, other animals and nearly *all* human beings are really rather super, I decided. Pony-mad, we'd been. And pony-mad we'd still go on being. But perhaps, after this, we'd also be pony-wise!

And with that great thought, I fell asleep!

Armada's Pony Parade

A host of exciting books about the wonderful world of horses and ponies are available in colourful Armada paperbacks. Each one, by a popular author and with a striking cover picture, makes a prize addition to your collection. Whether you have a pony of your own, or can only dream of one, they are all stories to thrill you.

Go galloping through the many pony adventures by the famous **Pullein-Thompson** sisters, **Christine**, **Diana** and **Josephine**.

Read about the escapades of Georgie and her beautiful chestnut pony, Spot, in the series by **Mary Gervaise**.

Ride into excitement and danger with Jackie, the daring young heroine of the pony series by **Judith Berrisford**.

And meet red-haired, rebellious Jinny Manders and her chestnut Arab mare, Shantih, in the 'Jinny at Finmory' books by **Patricia Leitch** in Armada's newest pony series.

Have fun building up your own
Pony Parade – start now!

Armada